First Comes Love
Series

second

chance

D1316525

ALSO BY KATIE KACVINSKY

Awaken

Middle Ground

First Comes Love

Dedicated to:

Adam Duritz

Your song lyrics inspired me to become a writer.
Is gray really your favorite color, too?
I hope we have that in common.

second chance

by

Katie Kacvinsky

Gray

I can't sleep tonight because memories are pooling in my mind like a lake and I'm floating face-down on the surface, trying to see the bottom.

Mostly, I'm thinking about a girl.

Which brings me to my latest theory:

I think falling in love should come with a warning label: CAUTION—side effects may include *breaking up*, accompanied by heartache, severe mood swings, withdrawal from people and life itself, wasted hours obsessing over bitter reflections, a need to destroy something (preferably something expensive that shatters), uncontrollable tear ducts, stress, a loss of appetite (Cheetos and Dr. Pepper exempt), a bleak and narrow outlook on the future, and an overall hatred of everyone and everything (especially all the happy couples you see strolling hand-in-hand, placed on your path only to exacerbate your isolation and misery). All above reactions will be intensified with the consumption of one or more alcoholic beverages.

What, me, bitter? Not at all. Just honest.

I turn the music up on my stereo and take a long drag off my joint. The smoke fills my lungs and I hold it in until I feel a soothing burn. I count the months it has been since I've heard from Dylan. I haven't seen her since she surprised me in Phoenix over Christmas, and I was naïve enough to think a long distance relationship could work. Now she's overseas gallivanting around Europe like a bird migrating from one scenic landscape to the next. She's slowly becoming my past, something like a dream and reality mixed. I forget where one ends and the other begins because the lines of memories are always a blur.

She flew to England with a family who hired her to chaperone their thirteen-year-old daughter for two months. They covered all of Dylan's traveling expenses and paid her a daily stipend. Only Dylan would fall into such a perfect situation, like fate for her is a waterfall that rushes her from one exciting adventure to the next with torrid speed because she never seems to slow down.

After her job commitment, Dylan stayed in Europe to backpack by herself. She sent me two postcards in the last four months. How thoughtful. It's comforting to know she spent about six minutes thinking of me in Melk, Austria and Munich, Germany. I've only spent about six hundred hours obsessing over her.

I'm assuming she met some hot Italian named Francisco or Alfredo. He probably has haunting dark eyes and chestnut brown hair that flows in the wine-infused wind. He seduced her with lines like, "I want to make love to you on the stars." And he can get away with sounding like an ass-clown just because he has an accent. How am I supposed to compete with *that*?

I take another hit from the inch of joint I have left and suck until the warmth of the burning paper teases my lips. I miss that heat. It feels like a kiss.

Francisco or Alfredo is probably kissing Dylan right now on a piazza that overlooks his forty acre family vineyard or his private beach front property along the Aegean Sea. I can see their future as plain as a European honeymoon brochure: He proposes to her on top of the Spanish Steps in Rome. They marry on a yacht while the sun sets below the Mediterranean. Something incredibly lame and romantic like that. Lamesauce, as Amanda and I used to call it. All I know is the European-love-affair would explain how Dylan has so easily forgotten to call her boring old American boyfriend. No sexy accent. No exotic past. I love to grill out, play baseball, and quote Ron Burgundy. That's my idea of culture.

Angry would be one word to describe my current state of mind. It's part of the getting-over-your-ex grieving process. It begins with heartbreak, followed closely by denial. Then comes a little resentment. Loathing. Mega-loathing. At last, anger sets in, and it fuels you to do what I've finally done: Throw yourself a pity party, get stoned for four months and move the hell on. It's healthy, organic rehab for only $99 a month, brought to you by Mexico. Pot has become my new best friend. It's a natural sleep aid and a much appreciated brain-numbing supplement that helps turn my life into a joke instead of something I have to try and make sense out of.

Dylan used to be my drug. When I was with her I was funnier, crazier, smarter and more creative—this person it felt so effortless to be. Meeting her last summer was like pulling on a favorite sweatshirt, worn and smooth and familiar, like she was sewn for me. The seams of her personality aligned perfectly with mine. We meshed.

Then why, in her absence, do I change? Why do I go back to being the *old* me? The one that judges everything, that sees the world through cynical eyes? Was I just faking my way through that whole summer with Dylan?

Maybe it was never me all along.

Or, maybe, when you meet the right person, it's like meeting a piece of yourself that you never knew existed because somebody had to open it up for you. Pull it out of you. Point it out to you. Is it true you need another person to be complete?

Well, I know one thing for sure. I won't fall in love that easily again. The next time around I'm going to be careful. I'm going to take it slow and wait until the timing is perfect.

No more heartache.

It's time to stop mulling over the past. I need to focus on the present. I'm going to put one hundred percent of my energy into my friends, roommates, baseball, school, parents—my life. Dylan gets zero percent.

That story is over.

Finished.

The end.

Dylan

I stretch out on the leather train seat and sip the thick, rich coffee Europe's famous for. I open my journal to a blank, white page. The paper looks like a canvas spread out, waiting for me to create a painting with words. Lately I've been thinking about love because it charges me and surrounds me and I crave it, follow it, live for it. Love is the only drug that's healthy to overdose on.

Which brings me to my random thought for the day:

I think falling in love should come with a warning label: CAUTION—side effects may include sporadic singing in public (specifically Celine Dion covers), emotional intoxication, constant fool grinning, stomach flipping, eye twinkling, heart palpitations, sweaty hands, jittery feet, lack of sleep, giddiness, deep sighs of contentment, sexual fantasizing, uncontrollable bouts of happiness, and the need to help everyone else around you fall in love so they can experience this blissful state. Do not attempt to operate heavy machinery under the influence of love, due to lightheadedness and daydreaming.

I close my journal and take a bite of a chocolate bar that's cold from sitting next to the drafty train window. Chocolate has become my new best friend. It's sweeter and creamier than chocolate in the U.S. Each bite is like dressing your mouth in sugary velvet. It's almost as good as kiss. Maybe that's why I crave it—it's a dietary supplement for when I'm away from Gray.

I peer out the window into a dark landscape dusted with lights in the distance, the city of Prague hovering in front of my fingers. I press my hand against the cold glass and try to connect the dots of the city skyline. Traveling gives me this natural high, like all my senses are heightened down to the end of my fingertips. I crave it like food, as if it's what propels me forward, what nourishes my body. Traveling is like leaving one world that's black and white and walking into another one drenched in color because everything is so new it becomes enchanting.

The train starts to slow down as it approaches Prague's station, and my feet tap anxiously on the ground. I can't sit still. Maybe it's the air—cold and dense and rich with mystery and texture. Maybe it's the sense of this new city I'm about to meet, like a stranger I want to get to know. Maybe it's the third cup of coffee I've had in the last hour.

It's amazing to think where adventure can lead when you trust your crazy ideas, when you're bold enough to look at only what lies ahead of you. I don't want the normal life. I don't want to go to college because it's the next practical step, just to join the pack, just to follow a leader. I don't want to sit inside a room under fluorescent lights and study and read and memorize other people's ideas about the world. I want to form my own ideas. I want to experience the world with my own eyes.

I'm not going to follow my old friends to avoid the effort of making new ones. I don't want to settle for any job just to get a paycheck, just to pay rent, just to need furniture and cable and more bills and be tied down with routine and monotony. I don't want to own things because they'll eventually start to own me.

Most importantly, I don't want to be told who I am or who I should be. I want to find myself—the bits and pieces that are scattered in places and in people waiting to meet me. If I fall down, I'll learn how to pick myself up again. You need to fall apart once in a while before you understand how you best fit together.

Few people understand what to make of me.

Except for one.

The more people I meet, the more I'm realizing how rare it is to find someone who lets you be yourself. Who never tries to hold you back, but watches you ride out the wave of intensity and see where it takes you. Gray never held me back. He was like a drug. He lit me up like a catalyst, and I can't go a day without thinking about him. Half of my journal entries are addressed to him. I take most of my pictures just so I can show him the places I've been. I've never missed anyone before. I try not to dwell on past memories; instead I focus on making new ones. But now I realize that distance is like a test. If you miss someone, it means you love him. It's that simple.

I can't wait to see him again and tell him our story is just beginning.

Growing.

Destined for happily ever after.

I lean my forehead against the cool train window and watch the city lights blink past me in the dark sky. My shoulders rock forward as the train grinds and brakes to a stop.

I stretch my sore legs and roll my luggage into a filthy train station, but I'm filthy too, so I can't complain. I grin at the atmosphere around me, the clattering sounds of languages I can't understand, the bustle of passengers, people moving along with me like we're all just cells, pushing our way together through a giant artery. I love meeting a city for the first time at night and seeing it dressed up with lights. It gives me time to imagine the rest of it before it greets me in daylight.

I head towards the street entrance, hail a cab, and find myself on a cobblestone street in front of the Czech Inn Hostel. Even though we meet for the first time and I'm thousands of miles from anyone I know, I feel like I'm home.

Gray

I wake up the next morning to the sound of birds that have unfortunately chosen the balcony outside my door for music rehearsal. Their soprano voices perform a song I imagine is titled, "Let's Annoy the Shit out of Gray." While they chirp and sing and whistle to the world, I roll over on my back and let out a long sigh. I've officially decided fish are my favorite animal because they're quiet and don't arouse me from a rare sleep.

The sun peers through the window blinds and paints narrow streaks of yellow light across my bed. I stare up at the ceiling, rub my eyes and wish I could fast forward through today. Since my twin sister Amanda passed away two years ago, my birthday is just a reminder that some parts of me are only half here. Death has a way of breaking you into pieces. You manage to put yourself back together, but in an odd alignment. Something will always feel off-center.

My roommates don't know today is my birthday. I haven't told anyone because I don't want to be congratulated. It's my second birthday without her. And I'm supposed to celebrate?

I kick off my covers and grab the nearest T-shirt lying next to my bed. I pull it over my head and throw on a pair of jeans. I run my fingers through my dark, curly hair but it's a lost cause to try and tame my morning afro, so I slide a UNM baseball hat on backwards. I brush my teeth and meet my reflection in the mirror to see streaks of dark purple under my eyes from the lack of sleep.

I head downstairs, and Miles is sitting in the kitchen eating a bowl of cereal and studying. His shoulders lean over a pile of notes spread out on the table. He looks up when I walk in, and there's an edge to his eyes. I open up the cupboard and grab some Pop Tarts.

Miles clears his throat. "Gray, do you mind not smoking pot in the house?" he asks. "I could smell it in my room last night."

I glance at him over my shoulder and apologize as I slip the Pop Tarts into the toaster. He exhales a long breath and I turn to face him, waiting for the lecture. Miles has a huge heart and he's become a good friend, but sometimes his need to be the paternal voice of the team is a buzz kill. Miles admits he's clueless about a lot of things, most of all women, but one area where you can't doubt his knowledge and dedication is baseball. Our household abides by one rule: baseball comes first. Those words should hang over our front door, just to warn people. Baseball comes before sleep and school and friends and girlfriends. Bubba and Todd, my other roommates, are happy to oblige, but I've become the black sheep of the team for daring to have interests outside the baseball field.

Miles frowns. He's clearly disappointed in me, and I can understand why. We're supposed to stay clean during the season. No drinking, no smoking. We're not supposed to show up at house parties or be out at the bars. On game nights we have a curfew.

"When are you going to give that up?" he asks me.

I shrug. "It helps me sleep," I say.

"It's Saturday. We have a game in a few hours," he tells me, as if I forgot.

"I'm not pitching this game," I remind him. Coach Clark rotates the starting pitchers, so I only throw every third game.

"That's not the point," Miles says. "We signed an athletic agreement."

"No one actually follows it," I argue. I point out Bubba still chews all the time.

Miles ignores this. "We sign it for a reason. Somebody wrote those rules."

"Somebody who doesn't understand moderation," I argue.

He shakes his head and eats another spoonful of cereal. I tell him I've cut way back, which isn't exactly true. I still smoke every night. And most mornings.

"You're supposed to be one of the best pitchers in the conference this year," he reminds me. "I don't want you to throw it all away because you're depressed."

I stare back at him. "I'm not depressed."

"Gray, you've perfected the art of sulking. If you need to talk about it, I'm here. But there are other ways you can deal with it."

I pull my Pop Tarts out of the toaster and burn the tips of my fingers. I throw them on a napkin. "Thanks a lot," I say.

"Look how far you've come since you've been here," he reminds me. "Coach was going to red-shirt you this year, but you're throwing better than any pitcher on the team."

Miles is right. I became the team's number one starting pitcher by the time we hit conference games this spring. Coaches and reporters predict I'll only get better. In interviews, everybody asks me my secret for success. Is it my die-hard dedication? My rigorous training schedule? My dream of playing pro?

In all honesty, I don't really think about it. Baseball's just a game. It isn't my life. It doesn't define me. At the end of the day, it's just a sport I love to play. It was the perfect excuse to get out of Phoenix, to go to college, to be part of a team, and most importantly, to move on with my life. I think the fact that I don't consider baseball the meaning of life and death and everything in between, like most of the guys on my team, gives me an advantage. I never get nervous before games. I never feel pressure or tense up. I throw technically perfect because pitching is one of the only parts of my life where I have complete control. I stand on top of the mound and for those sacred few hours, my life is fenced off. I can finally stop thinking and just be entirely in the moment.

"It's just a game, Miles," I say. I walk out of the kitchen, and let the screen door slam behind me. The morning air is cool, but the sun's warm on my skin. I put my headphones on and head down the block towards the the Brew House, a neighborhood café overrun with college students. It's also home to one of my best friends.

I walk up the front steps and pass a few girls on their way out the door that say hi to me and I nod back. I'm used to strangers recognizing me all over campus, calling me by my first name, even though I've never seen them before. Lenny's working behind the counter. She looks up from her newspaper crossword puzzle and welcomes me with a bored grin. Her real name is Linda (she confided this to me in trusted secrecy). It might be the biggest misfire in all of naming history. *Linda* is someone who coordinates food drives and charity events. *Linda* marries Sherman, and they have two kids. *Linda* works out at Curves and chairs the neighborhood garden club. *Linda* swaps recipes online, cuts coupons from the Sunday paper, and bargain shops at garage sales.

Lenny, meanwhile, sticks to a wardrobe of T-shirts featuring rock bands from the late seventies, rides her skateboard to work, and has a loop pierced through her plump bottom lip. Makeup would probably jump off of her face in fear if she ever tried to apply it. The only thing feminine about her is her long, thick black hair which she keeps tied back in a messy clip to restrain all the "stupid ass curls" that she argues is her genetic betrayal. Lenny is no nonsense, hates small talk, loves an argument and plays the insult game very well, so we've become fast friends.

"You look a little gray today, Gray," she says, taking in my sullen face.

"Thanks, *Linda*," I shoot back.

"Life getting you down, or are you just hormonal?"

I narrow my eyes and raise my voice. "That reminds me, did you get that autographed copy of Hillary Duff's album yet? I know you were so excited when you won it on eBay."

Lenny tightens her lips at this blow, but I interrupt our daily squabble to hit her with the truth.

"It's my birthday," I say. She blinks with surprise and fidgets with the pen next to her crossword puzzle. She knows enough about my past to understand why I'm not happy about it.

"Maybe I should have bypassed the morning insults," she offers, her way of apologizing.

"Hey, don't change your customer service standards just for me." She smiles, since she could care less about waiting on over-caffeinated college students. She's been roped into managing the Brew House, and the money's good enough to keep her away from getting her nursing degree. She's also living with her mom and helping to pay bills because her dad, whom her mom never married, was detained and sent back to Mexico three years ago for being an illegal immigrant. Lenny has light skin and her mom's small nose and angled chin, but her dark eyes, long lashes and black hair come from her dad. I tell her she could be attractive if she smiled a little more often. She tells me the same thing. Our friendship includes making fun of people as much as possible, sharing the occasional joint, and watching Christopher Guest films, because we can appreciate the art of turning life into one long mockumentary.

I ask Lenny for coffee, and she raises her eyebrows since I usually order juice. She fills a cup and sets it down on the counter.

"This one's on me," she says. I mumble thanks and tell her I'll be outside, where I meet her every morning for her cigarette break.

I walk down the street to the end of the block, sit on the curb, and toast to the sun with my cup. I take a sip and wonder if there's coffee in heaven. I wonder if there's an atmosphere, or if you even need to breathe. I wonder if you float everywhere, or walk, or drive, or if they have fuel emission laws for cars. I wonder if I'm still high from last night.

The coffee tastes strong and bitter, and it burns going down, but I drink it to honor Amanda, who drank about five cups a day. I turn on my phone to find two missed calls from my parents. I call my mom and it goes straight to her voicemail.

"Hi Mom, it's me. I'm sitting outside drinking coffee and thinking of Amanda. I hope you're feeling all right today. I love you."

I call my dad and leave the same message on his cell phone. I'm relieved they don't answer. I don't want to hear that bittersweet edge in their voice, like they're happy to hear from me, but we all know who they would give every ounce of their blood to hear from one last time.

I snap the phone shut as Lenny sits next to me on the curb.

"You want to talk about it?" she asks.

I shake my head. She pulls out a lighter and sparks her cigarette, but once she exhales I can tell it's a joint. She hands it to me and smiles.

"To Amanda," she says.

I look at the joint in her fingers and it's tempting. I can see Miles' disapproving face, reminding me I have a game today. But I could use a distraction. On a day like today, it's more medicinal than recreational. I'm willing to sacrifice a little lung tissue to settle my mind. I can spare a few brains cells—I think too much as it is. I grab the joint, take a long drag and pass it back. I mentally give myself a hard slap on the side of the head because my split second decisions tend to lean on the stupid side.

"You just missed your fan club," Lenny informs me. She tells me Amber McAssEasy and Valerie Slimslutty (nicknames she coined for volleyball players that have chased me in the past) came in this morning asking about me. She tells me they want the 411 on who I'm dating. She tells me she's sick of being the public portal into my dating life, or lack thereof.

I smile and tell her if it helps, to go ahead and validate one of the ongoing rumors circulating about me.

Lenny laughs and starts to list all the theories on campus explaining my single status (mostly originating from volleyball team gossip). Ever since I made the mistake of kissing Amber McCafrey at a party last year, but passed up the chance to sleep with her, I've been accused of many things.

"Let me see," Lenny says and leans back on her palms. "What's the latest theory?"

I take another hit instead of answering her.

"First, there's the gay rumor," she says.

I nod because I've heard that one numerous times. Lenny knows the long and exhausting Dylan saga, so I don't have to explain that one.

"There's also the one about you having a tiny penis."

Like anyone on this campus would know. "It's not about size, it's about stamina," I say.

"I've heard you're a virgin, and you're saving yourself," she continues, as if I'm enjoying this particular conversation. "Oh, and supposedly you have an erectile dysfunction."

I take an unnecessarily long drag and choke out the smoke. When I get my voice back, I shake my head. "You know what, Lenny? You really know how to cheer a guy up."

She stubs the joint out on the curb. When I stand up, the full affect of the pot hits me. I wobble on my feet a little until I catch a tree trunk for balance.

"Wow," I say. "That's pretty potent." I rub the back of my neck and confess I have to be at the ball park in an hour. Lenny blinks up at me, then she falls back on the grass and we both bust up laughing.

I walk back to the house, and I'm slowly climbing up the steps of the front porch when my cell phone rings. It's Coach Clark. It's not uncommon for him to call us on game days for a private pep talk, but I'm not pitching today so I start to wonder.

"Hello?"

"Gray," his loud voice rumbles over the phone. I pull the phone away from my ear. Do coaches ever stop shouting?

"How's your arm feeling?" he barks.

It feels wonderful, like it's floating, actually.

"Fine," I say.

"Good. I just wanted to give you a heads up. Pat's got some stomach virus so it looks like you'll be starting today. Hopefully he'll be back for tomorrow's game."

I have cotton mouth from the pot, and I'm high, and it almost sounds funny to hear this, like this is Lenny messing with me. I glance at the caller ID again, just to make sure, but Coach's name is spelled out on my screen, loud and clear. I can feel my heart start to hammer. I adjust the rim of my hat and clear my throat.

"What kind of a virus?" I ask. Tell me this isn't happening. Can't he just take some Pepto Bismol and suck it up?

"It came on pretty fast. Poor kid can't make it out of the bathroom."

"What about Richie?"

"No, I don't think he's ready. His shoulder's still tight. I want somebody consistent out there. What do you think?"

I tell Coach it sounds great and hang up the phone. I look up and try to focus on some of the branches in the tree above me, but I can't tell which is swaying—the branch or my head. I want to laugh because my depth perception is shot.

God, you really must hate me.

***

Isotopes Park is packed with fans, and we're playing our biggest rival, New Mexico State. I glance over my shoulder at the scoreboard, lit up in neon advertisements.

We're down by five runs and the bases are loaded in the bottom of the fourth inning. I can hear the frustration humming around the stadium. Fans are starting to boo me off the field and even our mascot, Lobo Louie, is hanging his wolf head. I'm ready for the DJ to start playing funeral music in between innings. Outside of right field, where people usually stretch out on blankets and relax on the grass, I notice fans are standing, arms crossed, bodies rigid, staring at the culprit who's ruining their Saturday afternoon. Me.

I take a deep breath and make a concerted effort to focus. I walked the last two players, and I've just succeeded in throwing the most consecutive wild pitches in my baseball career. I'm trying to concentrate, but no matter how hard I throw, my body feels like it's moving in slow motion.

I can just imagine what the radio announcers are saying in the press box: "Well, folks, if you just tuned into today's game, we're watching Gray Thomas confirm a baseball theory: pitchers perform poorly on pot."

In the dugout, half the team is sitting down, cowering in the shade, and the rest are leaning over the fence, fuming. The guys hate me. I know they suspect what's wrong. They saw how bloodshot my eyes were in the locker room. Miles won't even look in my direction. I stare out at the Sandia Mountains and try to relax, but the mountains loom and cower and the peaks look jagged like teeth, like a mouth getting ready to scream.

I turn back to home plate. Focus, Gray. Just get this guy out. Finish off the worst game of your life, put it behind you, learn from your incredibly stupid mistake and move on. Oh, yeah, and move Lenny to number one on your shit list.

I stare down the batter, but he just grins back at me. He isn't scared. He has three balls and one strike. He's waiting for me to throw another wild pitch so he can trot safely to first base and bring another runner home. It's almost impossible to throw a fast ball when my arm feels like it's a feather that wants to float away in the wind and land in a field full of nachos and cheese sticks surrounded by waterfalls pooling into a river of ranch dressing.

Just when I'm about to throw, Coach calls a timeout and stalks onto the field. He looks like he's ready to throw me to a pack of mountain lions. He runs his hands over his thick, spiky gray hair and takes off his sunglasses. His dark brown eyes are furious.

"What the hell are you doing, Gray? You know how this guy works. You throw him sliders and he swings low every time. It's an easy out. Why are you trying to throw wide? He's not going to swing at that."

I shrug because that's the problem. I'm not thinking. "Sorry, Coach."

"What's the matter with you?" He suspects something so I tell him. I play my trump card.

"It's my birthday," I say. The look on my face says the rest. I don't have to remind him who shares my birthday, that this is one of the hardest days of the year for me, and that it was a struggle just to get out of bed.

His eyes narrow as he watches me, and I see some of the anger drain from his face. But there's still suspicion on the surface. "You should have told me you couldn't play when I called you," he says.

"I thought I could pull it out," I say, and I leave out the fact that being stoned doesn't exactly help.

Coach thinks about this for a second. "You want me to take you out?" he asks. This is a gamble. I'd rather pitch an awful game than give up. I shake my head and tell him

I'll finish off the inning. He slams the ball back in my glove.

"Get this guy out and then we'll talk," he says.

My heart's drumming nervously in my chest, and a cold sweat creeps over my arms and neck. Too many people are moving in the stands. There's too much noise. I get nauseous for a second and think I'm going to throw up. I take a shaky breath and glare at the batter. I can see the shadow of his eyes underneath his helmet. He swings the bat in circles behind his shoulder and waits for the pitch.

I roll the leathery ball in my fingers until I like where the laces line up. *You're mine.*

I wind up and throw a curve ball a little outside the plate and forget to make it a slider. The batter swings and cracks the bat against the ball. I wince and follow its path in the sky, deep into center field where it hits the wall and bounces to the ground. He makes it to second base. Two more runners make it home. Coach pulls me from the game and a freshman pitcher relieves me, closing off our loss. Most of the fans leave before the game comes to an embarrassing end.

***

Back in the clubhouse, Coach calls me into a side office. Miles is sitting in there with him so either he ratted me out or he's trying to throw me a life-line. Miles has a lot of respect on the team, and Coach looks to him to be a leader. I sit down and pull my baseball cap as low over my head as it will go. I press the tips of my fingers together and wait. There's a quiet few seconds while Coach studies me. He rolls a pencil back and forth on his desk.

"I'm having some doubts about your dedication to this team, Gray," he says. "But Miles is trying to convince me I'm wrong about that."

I glance at Miles, but his eyes are on the floor. Coach is silent again, just to terrify me. And it's working. I realize I might have just played my last college baseball game.

"Listen," he says, "I know you're dealing with something the rest of these guys haven't been through. But I'm not making excuses for you. So, here's my question. Is getting high before a baseball game a one time mistake, or is this becoming a problem?"

I take a deep breath and try to find my voice. Why is it that until you come close to losing something, you don't understand how much you want it? Need it?

I look back at Coach. "It won't happen again. I swear my life on it."

"Everyone's entitled to one mistake," he says. "One."

"That's all it was," I say quietly.

Coach sits back in his chair. "Do you need to talk to anybody about this? A psychologist?"

"No," I say. I tell him I've been seeing a counselor with my parents back in Phoenix.

He sits up straighter in his seat. "That was Phoenix. Maybe you should see somebody here."

I shake my head. "I'm doing better, Coach. Today was a mistake."

He eyes me skeptically. "I'm giving you a two game suspension. Then you're on probation the rest of the season." I nod quickly and tell him that's fair. "I don't think you see the severity of this, Gray," he warns me. "It could make the newspapers. I'll have to explain why my star pitcher isn't suited up. Something like this can kill any shot at a career. And I'll have to call your parents."

I stare back at him as his words hit me. I feel like I'm starring in the after school special: *The Higher You Get, the Lower You Fall: The Gray Thomas Story.* Except this isn't a joke. This is my real life I'm screwing with.

"Two things, Gray. One, if you don't think you can play, you need to communicate with me. I can't read your mind. Two, stay clean," Coach says. "I mean it. If I find out that you so much as look at a beer, or are in the same room as marijuana, then I'll have to cut you. I'm not going to waste my time on guys that don't want to be here when there are hundreds of players that would kill to be in your spot."

I swallow and take his offer. "Got it."

I stand up and summon enough self-esteem to lift my head and walk out of the room. I open the door and Miles follows behind me. Coach yells for Richie to come in and talk to him. His office door slams closed and the next thing I know I'm slammed against a locker, with Travis Taylor's face inches from mine. He pushes his hands against my chest. I can smell anger on his breath. The metal locker jam is digging into my shoulder, but I don't try to stop him. I don't have any fight left.

"You stupid, selfish piece of shit. You do something like that again and I'll kick you off the team myself," he says. Miles tries to pry us apart.

"Dude, let it go. Coach handled it."

"Stop changing his diapers, Miles. The kid's got to grow up sooner or later."

He turns his scowl back to me, and I keep my face level with his. His green eyes are smoldering with anger.

"You want to curl up and die, be my guest. But you're not taking the team down with you," he says. Todd and Bubba and Miles are standing close by, but they don't step in. I think Travis is speaking for everyone. The locker room is quiet as the rest of the guys turn to listen.

"He has a point, Gray," Todd says. "It's not just you. It's the whole team you're messing with."

My eyes narrow at the attack I'm getting in all directions. "Thanks for this thoughtful intervention guys," I say. "Are you going to give me a workbook I can fill out to help me find myself?"

Travis slams my back against the locker again.

"This is my life," Travis says. "This team is my shot at the pros, and I'll drop you before I let you screw up our season."

"Alright, back off," Bubba says, and he pulls Travis away from me. Bubba has four older brothers and claims to have a lifetime of experience breaking up fights. He's thicker than both of us and has tribal tattoos that curl around each of his biceps, which he can pull off because he's actually from a tribe.

Travis lets go of his grip on my shirt and stares me down. He grabs his duffel bag but before he walks out the door he stops and turns to face me. There's still a death threat on his face.

"And as for your sister—"

My hands clench into fists. Now he's pushing it.

"Get over it. Move on, Gray. You're pathetic."

Before my heart takes another beat my hands are on him and with the force I use to push him, we both fall hard to the ground. I throw a fist that lands on his jaw and there's a loud smack when bone meets bone. His fist flies and I take a blow to the side of my face. The contact makes light explode behind my eyes. A dozen hands try to pry us apart. I slam my knuckles into stomach, and he takes another swing that hits my mouth. There's a flash of heat from the punch and I can taste blood on my lips.

Someone's grabbing my waist and I'm getting pulled off of him. Voices are shouting, but the sound barely penetrates through the fire raging in my head. Bubba has my arms pinned back and I'm pushing to get free.

"You can say anything you want about *me* Travis, but the next time you insult Amanda, I'm taking you out," I yell. The hate pouring from my eyes must be making me blind because I don't see Coach until he starts yelling.

"That's enough," Coach barks at us. "When the hell did my team turn into a bunch of middle school girls? Gray, go home. Travis, I want you in my office. Now."

Bubba lets me go and Miles shoves me out of the locker room. He tells me to get in the car like he's my dad and I'm grounded. I slam the door shut and slump down into the backseat, wiping the blood off my mouth with my T-shirt. I wonder if my life can get any worse.

Dylan

Can my night get any worse? A half hour ago, my luggage was stolen at the train station. I'm soaking wet and freezing cold after running three blocks in rain and sleet. Now, I'm stranded in the middle of Switzerland, and it's past midnight.

"Look, I have a reservation," I insist and smack my receipt on the counter for proof. "There is no way you can be full."

The manager of the Alpine Hostel in Interlaken stands across the bar from me. He looks younger than I am and his long, curly blond hair bounces like springs when he shakes his head. He says something in a British accent.

"What?" I yell over the shouts and music inside the bar, which doubles as a check in lobby for the hostel.

"You're supposed to call to confirm the room, love," he says. "It's our policy, since you didn't put down a deposit." He informs me that I was supposed to call twenty-four hours in advance to confirm the reservation. He points out the fine print on my receipt. I follow his finger along the words. Fine print, I decide, is bullshit.

"What are you saying, Mr. Alpine? You're going to throw me out on the street?" He ignores my question to fill a pitcher of beer for a customer, because that's more important than my current state of homelessness.

I breathe out a heavy sigh and sit down on a bar stool. Normally I love a challenge, but I'm really not in the mood to be stranded on a rainy night in a foreign country. I'm surrounded by a mob of partiers and smoke so thick I could be sitting inside a burning building. All I want is a warm, quiet bed. I wipe wet strands of hair off my face and stick out my bottom lip, forcing it to tremble for a dramatic effect. The manager isn't fooled.

"We're booked up," he says and then he grins. "But you're a cute girl. I'm sure you can finagle your way into some bloke's room." He winks at me and I frown. Does he think I'm going to put out, just for a place to crash? I know I'm an American, but despite the rumors, we're not *all* easy.

I wrap my stone-washed jean jacket tighter around my chest and my teeth chatter. I inherited this jacket at a flea market in London. It loudly displays the British flag on both the front and back and it's so ugly the person working the booth gave it to me for free. I feel a special bond with the coat, like we're both underdogs, just looking for people to love us for who we are. I know it's strange to feel an emotional connection to a garment, but strange seems to summarize my thinking process in general. The inside of the coat is even lined with red, white and blue stripped flannel. Bonus.

I drum my fingers on top of the bar and mentally sort through my cash. I have barely enough money to pay for food and lodging for the next two weeks, let alone budget for a new wardrobe. Almost everything I own in my life was in that stupid luggage. All my clothes. An old T-shirt I stole from Gray that I sleep with every night and still smells like him. Souvenirs I bought for all my family and friends. Three journals I filled during the trip. A painting I bargained for from an artist in Prague. A poster of the England Cricket team I bought for Gray. Clean, dry underwear.

I'm comforted to know I still have my camera, money and ID's in my backpack. I try to count my blessings. I have my health, minus all this second hand smoke. I'm alive. I'm not in a gang. But for the first time since I've been traveling, I want to go home. I want to see the calm eyes of someone I trust. Gray's eyes. I want to lie on his warm chest in the dark and turn the music up and my thoughts down.

My thoughts are interrupted when a guy wearing a shiny soccer jersey falls against me, blowing a mouthful of beer breath in my face. He apologizes to my boobs. Nice. I shove him off me and he teeters on his feet until he catches the bar ledge.

"Do you know where else I can stay?" I ask the manager. He tells me the whole city's full-up for an air show in town. My head sinks down to my arms and I rest my forehead on the bar. When I let out an exhausted groan, he sets a beer down in front of me.

"This one's on me, love," he says. "Looks like you can use a pint."

"Thanks," I say and slam half the beer. I look around the smoky space and see a blue couch in the corner of the room. Half the upholstery is ripped off and there could be a rat infestation going on, but I have a feeling that it's going to be my bed tonight. Just as I reach this conclusion, a young girl and guy crash down on the couch, their hands pawing at each other's faces and lips pressed together. He climbs on top of her and she pulls his shirt halfway up his back.

I guess I won't be using that couch after all. A deep yawn escapes my throat and my eyelids feel like weights are pulling them closed. Despite the music and the noise, I start to nod off at the bar.

A girl suddenly slams an empty pint down next to me and I jump in my stool, almost falling over. She looks about my age, with an army cap pulled low over short brown hair. She has a round face and full red lips and she's nudging away the same drunk guy that fell on me. I notice she's talking in an American accent. She glances at me and her huge, brown eyes meet mine. She takes in my drooping eyelids and the fact that it's taking considerable effort for me to hold my head up.

"Are you okay?" she asks.

I consider this word. "Okay's a vague descriptor," I say. "If you consider *okay* as in all my limbs are currently attached to my body and I'm not suffering from a terminal illness, than yes, I'm okay. If, however, you take into account that I'm homeless, soaking wet, all my luggage was stolen, I'm wearing the only pair of underwear I own, and I'm in a foreign land where I know no one, then no, I guess I'm not okay."

I slam the rest of my pint and she's still standing there, studying me. "Enough about me," I say. "What's your story?" I stare back at her and grin because it's just nice to have company. She smiles and tells me she's out here visiting her grandmother, but she's from the States.

I picture her grandmother's quaint, quiet cottage, probably nestled between pine trees. I imagine it's clean and quiet, with a little stone fireplace that's lit right now, crackling and filling the room with a toasty warm glow. I try not to let my jealousy show. Why can't I have relatives that live in Europe? All my family lives in Wisconsin, Iowa and North Dakota. Probably the three most unexciting places on Earth.

"You look exhausted," she says.

I glance over at the blue couch. It's empty again and looking more abused than ever. I wonder out loud if the cushions will give me head lice. I wonder if head lice burns or itches or both. I wonder if it looks like dandruff.

"Come on," she says and grabs the damp sleeve of my jacket.

"Where are we going?"

"You're staying with me. I'm not going to leave you in a bar all alone. Girls have to watch out for each other."

I stand up and grab my backpack. I don't know who this girl is or if she's psychotic or a serial killer or trying to rob me of my last remaining possessions, but at this point I'm too tired to care.

***

The next morning, I'm treated to tea and homemade cinnamon bread. Catherine's grandmother is seventy-five years old, but has the energy of a teenager. Her curly hair is dyed bright red and she wears a loose, black dress that sways in the air with her movements. She runs a B&B out of her house and goes by Madame Kuntz to her customers. There's an older, quiet Japanese couple dining with us in the parlor and both of their faces are glued to travel books and brochures.

Catherine's grandmother made it her mission this morning to piece together a make-shift wardrobe for me. She gave me an old, giant duffel bag out of her hall closet and let me choose from a crate full of clothes left by other travelers. I inherit a blue hooded sweatshirt with HAWAII spelled on the front in white letters, socks, a few V-neck T-shirts, and a couple pairs of jeans. I also acquire a pair of silver flip flops that fit my absurdly long feet, and a pair of brown corduroy pants that are too short and rise just above my ankles.

I take a sip of black tea and look out the picture window in front of the table. The Alps stretch out in the distance, white and brilliant and shining like glittering diamonds against a clear blue sky. The snowy peak of Jungfrau stands out against the others and its giant presence makes all my problems dissolve. How can I dwell on what I lack when, looking out at this skyline, I have everything? I'm reminded that possessions are meant to be temporary. Material things are easily replaced. The important things people can never steal—love, hope, trust, faith—these things are sewn inside of us, tattooed like ink inside our hearts.

I look around the room and think it's strange that sometimes you have to lose what you have in order to gain what you need. Sometimes you need to be desperate to be reminded angels exist. And there's nothing more rejuvenating to the spirit than to fall asleep to the pattering of rain at night and wake up to a clear, blue sky. It's the greatest omen in the world.

I help myself to another thick, warm piece of buttery cinnamon toast. Catherine tells me she's heading back to the States tomorrow, but her grandmother has an open room if I need a place to stay.

"Where's home?" I ask her.

"Albuquerque," she says. I almost choke on a mouthful of bread and take a huge gulp of tea to flush it down.

"New Mexico?" I ask, when I get my breath back. She grins and says she's pretty sure there's only one Albuquerque.

"Do you go to school there?" I ask. She shakes her head and tells me she dropped out last year. She teaches guitar lessons and is the lead singer in her band, Chuck's

Angel. They're waiting for their drummer to graduate so they can set up a road trip tour.

"I live close to campus," she says. "My roommates all go to UNM."

I smooth out the napkin on my lap. "I hear it's a good school," I say. She nods and says its okay, if you like the whole college thing.

"Have you ever been to a baseball game?" I blurt out before I can hold it back. "I mean, my cousin's thinking about playing there, so I was wondering if the team's any good." I sip my tea as if this is a typical conversation to have in Switzerland over breakfast.

I expect Catherine to roll her eyes. She looks about as knowledgeable of college baseball as Madame Kuntz, but she surprises me and tells me they have a great team.

"I've been to a few games," she says. "One of my friends is a jersey chaser, so she's dragged me to more than one sporting event."

"Do you know any of the players?" I ask and try to keep my tone casual. She shakes her head and tells me she isn't into athletes. Too cocky.

"I know one of their girlfriends, Liz. She works at my favorite boutique downtown. She's dating Todd Richards and he lives with some other players, Miles somebody, and Gray." I wonder if she notices me flinch when she says Gray's name. I stare across the table at Catherine. Out of all the people to run into last night, this musician from Albuquerque has heard of the love of my life?

She looks at my dazed expression and asks me if I'm alright.

I nod, slowly, and decide it's time to confess. "Okay, the truth is, one of the players on the team just happens to be my soulmate and future husband."

She sets her cup down and grins at me. "Which one?"

"Gray," I say. "Gray Thomas. He's the love of my life and we're going to get married someday. When the timing's right," I inform her. I pour more hot water into my teacup.

Her eyebrows arch with surprise. "So you like the bad boys?"

"What?" I ask. Gray's sarcastic and cynical and a little brooding but—

"You didn't know he's on probation?"

I shake my head and ask her what she's talking about.

"Before I left the States, I heard he had some drug issues. A few weeks ago he threw an entire game high. He almost got kicked off the team." She smiles like she's impressed.

I frown as this news sets in. My perfect, sexy Gray is on probation for a being a stoner?

"You didn't know any of that was happening?" she asks, "and he's 'the love of your life?'"

"We haven't spoken in a few months," I admit. For the first time, I feel a pang of regret in my chest. It sinks in how much of Gray's life I'm missing out on. It's easy to be far away from the people you love when you think everyone's happy. But when you find out someone needs you and you can't be there, it makes the distance grow claws and teeth and start to gnaw at your heart.

Cat looks intrigued. "What I want to know is, if he's your soulmate, what are you doing backpacking alone in Switzerland?"

I rip off a corner of the toast and chew on it. "What do you mean?"

"Why aren't you together?" she presses. "Call me a hopeless romantic, but I think love's everything. It's up there with food and water and shelter and oxygen. I think you need it in order to survive. So if you're lucky enough to find love, why are you passing it up?"

I stare back at her as she talks about love like it's a buried treasure, like it's something you need to go on an archeological dig to uncover. I believe it's in endless supply. It's everywhere if you tap into it.

"I'm not passing it up. I just don't want to settle down right now. I'm only eighteen years old. Besides, I think you can bring love with you wherever you go," I say. "Love can wait for you."

She thinks about this for a few seconds. I watch her piecing my words together, like my refreshing wisdom is all starting to make sense.

"That makes absolutely no sense," she says. "Do you know how ridiculous you sound?"

My forehead creases.

"If you're in love with someone, you should be *with* him," Cat presses. "Or give him up. You can't have it both ways."

"Gray's okay with this," I argue. "He *gets* me. He knows I want to travel. We agreed to see each other when it works out, but we promised never to hold each other back."

She raises her eyebrows. "Are you sure about that? It's one thing to go to Europe for a few weeks, but you can't just leave for six months whenever you feel like it, and have him be okay with it. It's not fair to him." She registers the surprise on my face and raises her hands. "Sorry. I know it's none of my business. I can be a little opinionated."

I shake my head. "It's okay." Then an idea occurs to me. "Maybe my future self entered your body to give me crucial advice I need to hear in order to lead me down the right path."

Cat ignores me. "Listen, Dylan, you're awesome. I figured that out in about two seconds. But I've tried dating people like you, musicians that breeze through town. They're so easy to fall for because they're unique and inspiring, but it gets old really fast because you can never depend on those people."

I set my hands down on the table and look at her like she's giving me an ultimatum. "So, you're saying I should break up with him?"

She laughs at my question. "What do you mean, break up? What's there to break up? You're not even in a relationship. You haven't spoken to each other in months. You call that a relationship?"

I look down at my plate as her words sink in.

"I think you need to figure out what's more important to you, freedom, or Gray," she says.

***

Later that afternoon, I head downtown with my camera. My head and heart are sore from the honesty beating I took from Catherine and I need some air. I love the escape of getting outside and taking pictures. It helps me get out of my head and focus on things outside of me. One side of the street is crammed with hotels and people eating at outdoor restaurants. On the other side is a small city park that dissolves into an open green field with the view of the Alps towering in the distance.

I try to take a few pictures, but every time I lift the lens to my face, Cat's word echo through my head and I can barely see straight. I sit down on the curb, a few feet away from an outdoor café, and stare across the street at the grassy field next to the park.

My mom always tells me that you can't become who you're meant to be without planting roots. But maybe that's not me. Maybe I'll always be a girl that's flying. Except, I'm learning that eventually your feet need to touch the ground. You need to land and refuel.

Maybe Cat's right. Maybe it's time to settle down. My only questions are: Where, When, Why, and For How Long? Why are some of the tiniest questions in life the hardest to answer?

I study two women sitting at a café table a few feet away from me. They're meeting for a business lunch, immersed in conversation and pouring over notes and laptops between them. They're both wearing black heeled shoes with stylish black skirts and blouses with frilly collars that flip over their camisole sweaters. They look so content, so organized, so focused. I want to ask them: What is your secret? How do you know what you want to do with your lives?

I'm so amazed by people who know what they're passionate about, who have it all figured out in high school. They know they want to be doctors or teachers or artists. They remind me of trees—strong and tall and confident as they climb up to the sun. I never knew what I was good at in high school. I never had a teacher pull me aside and tell me I was talented, probably because teachers don't typically commend students for having a two-second attention span, daydreaming through class, or for talking more than they listen. And there aren't a whole lot of job listings for wandering travelers (I've looked).

I sigh and lean back on my hands and suddenly a giant, neon orange wing soars over the café's green awning above me. Its satin fabric stretches at least fifty feet in the air and tucked in the center is a small, black, human body. The whole creature looks part human, part plane, part butterfly. A blue kite glides in behind the orange one and they glissade back and forth, like they're sweeping a section of the sky. The orange glider touches down in the empty field across from me.

My hand instinctively reaches for my camera, but I'm out of film.

I do the next best thing.

I grab my journal out of my backpack and use a pencil to outline the shape of the kites, so I can safely store the image.

"Are you seeing this?" I ask to no one in particular and I'm answered by a young couple passing behind me on the sidewalk, both carrying breakfast croissants wrapped in paper.

"They're jumping off those cliffs," the guy answers me. He waves his finger at a rise of jagged hills behind the restaurant that frame the edge of the valley town. "They're just hang gliding," he points out, like it's no big deal.

I stare up at the cliffs towering thousands of feet into the sky. "That's such amazing trust," I say. "Can you imagine throwing your body off the side of a cliff and having faith something will catch you?"

I look between them and wait for an answer. They both stare at me like our eyes are seeing different things, which is a common response to most of my observations. But I barely notice their reaction because an image pops into my head. I think people can be like those wings, people can catch us and help us glide to a smooth landing after we jump and free fall from making crazy decisions. It makes me think of Gray, my human hang glider. It's a sign.

I spring to my feet, swing my backpack over my shoulder and half skip, half run down the sidewalk toward an Internet café. I almost trip over the curb when I cross the street because I'm still looking up at the sky. My heart's hammering as if I just experienced my own free fall. Suddenly hang gliders are everywhere. I see them in an older couple sitting on a bench, the woman using the man's shoulder as a pillow. I see them in kids holding hands to cross the street and friends leaning over table tops, talking and laughing. I don't doubt what I'm about to do because my split second decisions are always my best.

How did I not realize what my next move needs to be? That *he* is where I need to be?

I sprint up the stairs of the café entrance and walk inside a lobby that smells like sweat and dusty travelers. There's a line five people deep waiting to get on the available computers. I lean against the wall and grab my frayed, red wallet out of my backpack. I pull out the plane voucher for my return flight home, given to me by the family that flew me out to Europe four months ago. Has it seriously been four months?

I tap the voucher impatiently against my chest. Now I just have to come up with a memorable surprise plan. I could show up at Gray's front door wearing a giant red bow, like in those car commercials. Or, even better, I'll design a scavenger hunt and take him all over the city until it leads back to his bedroom, where I'll be waiting for him.

Naked.

I can already feel his arms around me, welcoming me home.

Gray

Lenny, Miles and I walk into the Velvet Room, a restaurant downtown that hosts live music every night. It's one of our first nights off in weeks. My suspension is over and I've pitched three winning games, so Miles has agreed to let me out, under his direct supervision. Lenny's taking us to see a local band called Chuck's Angel. They took a month-long break and now they're back to their regular Thursday night gigs.

We walk downstairs into the crowded bar and pay a five dollar cover charge. The basement room's dimly lit and the wide space has a few open tables in the back. The walls are covered in dark blue velvet, as well as the bar stools and seat cushions. The band has already started their set when we sit down. They have an acoustic, folk sound and Cat Parker's voice is low and breathy as if she has to push her notes out from deep in her chest. She's wearing a short skirt with dark tights and an army hat.

"She is hot," Miles says, gaping at her. I have officially given up guessing his type. A month ago he dragged me to a gymnastics meet to watch a girl who was five feet tall perform acrobatic feats to bad music. She moved with so much elasticity it was uncomfortable to watch. I'm pretty sure it was her flexibility that lured Miles. Cat Parker is the exact opposite, with her black combat boots and curvy shape.

When a waitress takes our order, Lenny asks if we want to split a pitcher and I tell her only if it's non-alcoholic beer.

"What? Don't you have a fake ID?" she whispers to me, and I remind her I'm on probation for the rest of my scholarship-endorsed life. Miles and I each order sodas.

"I thought your probation was for drugs?" she asks.

"Alcohol is a drug, Lenny," I say, although most people that live in a college town would argue that alcohol is as vital to consume on a daily basis as water. She points out she meant illegal drugs.

"I'm not twenty-one," I remind her. "It is illegal."

"Ugh, athletes," she mumbles.

Miles shushes us because Cat's speaking to the crowd. She thanks us for coming and introduces her band. I scan the audience and make eye contact with a cute brunette across the room. She smiles at me from the bar. She's wearing knee high black boots and a short skirt and it's pretty hot. I smile back.

Cat explains her next song is a cover and dedicated to an experience she had with an unexpected friend she made in Switzerland. She starts strumming her guitar and I recognize the riff for *Shelter From The Storm*. I wince a little because this song has always reminded me of Dylan.

"Is it my imagination," Lenny says, "Or is the bar slowly migrating in our direction?"

Miles and I look around at the room full of girls and I point out we're two of the only guys in the audience. Miles nods and says we should check out chick bands more often.

"Speaking of women," Miles says and looks at me, "whatever happened with that girl? Dana? You haven't mentioned her in a while."

"Dylan," I say. Just the word on my tongue makes the edges of my brain sizzle. I take a sip of my drink and shake my head. "That's over," I say. Lenny's mouth drops open and she reminds me I referred to Dylan as the love of my life.

"That was the pot talking," I inform her. "I think I also vowed eternal love for grilled cheese sandwiches and tater tots."

"The good ol' days," Lenny says with a smile. We're all quiet for a few minutes while we watch the band and absorb the sound. My mind starts to decompress; a natural reaction to live music. Cat begins another song, this one an original. Lenny glances sideways at me and asks if I'm seriously over Dylan. I nod and it doesn't feel forced.

"I haven't seen her since Christmas," I say, like that should explain it. Like time can erase feelings. "That was over four months ago."

"True love knows no boundaries," Lenny mocks.

"True love can take the hint someone in Europe forgot you exist," I say.

I glance around the bar. The room is filling with people. I notice a half dozen girls cuter than Dylan. They wear clothes that actually fit, they comb their hair and look presentable and I can see their fingernails painted in bright colors instead of embedded with dirt and sand and chewed off. These are real women. Dylan was just a big kid.

I try to think of a word that defines Dylan. She isn't cute. Or pretty. Or hot. She's like an abstract painting—something that catches your eye and forces you to stop and study it, but it's difficult to label what you see. All you know is you're staring at something unique. It's interesting for a while, but now I want a girl who attempts to be feminine, who's going to college and has realistic goals.

Besides, why waste my time wanting the one woman I can never have?

Lenny asks me what I would do if Dylan walked through the door, right now.

"What would you say if she walked up to our table and said she was passing through town?"

My eyes fall back on the girl across the room and she looks up at me and smiles. Game on. I set my glass down and look Lenny straight in the eyes, giving her the same intense gaze I give batters on the plate to remind them who's in control.

"I'd tell her to keep right on going," I say, and stand up to go talk to this girl.

Dylan

I'm so tired I'm pretty sure I could sleep standing up. Maybe I'll try. I haven't eaten a meal in twenty-four hours, except for a Rold Gold Snack Mix (ranch flavored) the airline so generously gave us as a complimentary snack to tide us over during the ten hour flight from Zurich to Chicago. Definitely satisfying.

As I stand in line to board my third flight, I try to remember where I am and where I've been in the last thirty hours. It started with a 5 a.m. train ride out of Interlaken to catch a 9 a.m. flight to Chicago. I didn't sleep a wink because two toddlers on the plane decided to have alternating meltdowns. I had a three hour layover before I caught a flight to Dallas. Now, only one hour and forty minutes of air travel separates me from Gray.

When I finally arrive at the airport in Albuquerque, my body moves with all the grace and coordination of a bag of lead. My lips are chapped, my eyes hurt, and my shoes smell so bad I consider throwing them away, but I'm too tired to untie the laces. I trip over my own feet on the way to the baggage claim and decide to take a short rest against the wall, next to the restrooms. I have to wait for my luggage, anyway.

***

Distant voices try to wake me up, but I refuse to open my eyes. If lack of sleep were an Olympic competition, I could have placed at least silver. So I deserve a nap. Their mumbling continues to stir the air around me. They sound French. Wait, am I in France? I can't remember.

"*Pas, merci*," I say without opening my eyes and swat my arm in the air. "*Aller-on.*" Wow. I'm impressed I remember the words for *no, thank you* and *go away* in my dazed subconscious.

"What is she saying?" I hear an elderly voice whisper.

"I think she's French," another woman answers.

Ugh, great. Wrong language. Where am I again? Germany?

"*Nicht, danke*," I groan.

"What was that?" someone asks.

"She must be from Europe."

I recognize the American voices and open my eyes to meet the concerned gaze of two gray-haired women leaning down and peering in my face. They step back, startled.

"Dear, we were worried about you," one of them says to me slowly as if she thinks I can't understand English. "You looked unconscious."

I pull myself up and press my hand against my forehead to try and ease a head rush that feels like someone is banging a metal hammer against the side of my head. I stare with a frown at the conveyer belt. There's my lowly duffel bag, still making its rounds like an old, abandoned dog waiting for someone to notice it.

"I must have fallen asleep," I say and rub my eyes. I blink and try to focus on the friendly faces that look concerned for my well-being.

"Is someone picking you up?" one of them asks me.

"Where am I?" I ask and I fast forward through the last few hours of my memory. Chicago? No. Dallas?

"Albuquerque, New Mexico in the United States of America," the old lady says slowly.

I slap my palm against my forehead. "That's it." And then it hits me. I'm here! After traveling over land, ocean, mountains, desert and experiencing way too much turbulence, I'm home. Only miles, minutes from Gray, who will take me in his arms and let me sleep for forty-eight hours and rip off my clothes and throw me down on the bed and act out my sexual fantasies and eat a huge plate of biscuits and gravy. Not necessarily in that order.

I grab a scrap of paper out of my pocket with Gray's address and tell these women I need a cab. One of them introduces herself as Margaret and insists on seeing me safely home. I smile and thank her. I get to my feet and waddle to the bathroom to brush my teeth and wash my face, which I discover has deep indents down the side of my cheek from sleeping on my backpack. I brush my teeth with my index finger because I'm too exhausted to look for my toothbrush. I'm so done with traveling for a while.

***

Margaret turns her old Cadillac onto Gray's street and I look around with a content smile. The off-campus housing is exactly how I imagined it. Old, two and three story homes sit close to each other under large maple trees that line the sidewalks. Students pedal by on bikes or walk along the sidewalk, clutching mugs of coffee. Mmm. Coffee. Guys are throwing footballs in the street and grilling out on front porches with beers in their hands and flip flops on their feet. I feel like I'm watching an infomercial advertising the diverse and happy student lifestyle at the University of New Mexico.

I ask Margaret to pull over when I see Gray's house. It's white with blue shutters framing the windows, has three stories, and looks like a giant birthday cake. Maybe I'm just hungry. If I were a giant I'd light candles on top of it and kick off my own welcome home party. I get out of the car and stretch while Margaret unlocks the trunk so I can grab my duffel bag. She hugs me and welcomes me once more to the United States. She assures me I'll love it here and that Americans are very friendly.

I fibbed a little bit and told her I was from Switzerland. She was so excited to help a foreigner—I didn't want to disappoint her. Margaret drives down the street and I wave goodbye. I cross the sidewalk and gaze up at his house. I try to guess Gray's window. If I lived here, I'd want the top room because they always have the low, slanting ceilings and this one has its own fire escape. Butterflies fill my stomach as I trudge up the porch steps and knock on the front door. I know sexy is the furthest word to describe my appearance and clean is far from my current state of hygiene, but I still hope Gray will at least wrap his arms around me. I knock on the door again, louder this time, but I'm answered by silence. I decide the porch will do just fine for a temporary bed and roll out my newly acquired airplane blanket, a souvenir I felt entitled to. Thanks, Delta.

I stretch the blanket on the wood porch and use my duffel bag as a pillow. I throw my blue hooded sweatshirt over my shoulders and pull the hood over my face to block out the light. I'll just relax for a few minutes. Just until I come up with a plan.

Gray

The four of us amble up the steps to the front door, getting home late from a three hour practice. It's past dinner and we're all starving. Todd suddenly stops in front of me at the top of the stairs and I almost run into him. Miles and Bubba run into me until the four of us are huddled in a human traffic jam. I follow Todd's startled gaze to the ground near his feet.

"Dude, we've got a homeless person on our porch," he says quietly and points to this girl, sprawled out on the floor like our address was recently listed as a shelter. She's got a blue Hawaii sweatshirt wrapped around her chest and a square, navy blue blanket spread out underneath her. She's using a tattered black duffel bag as a giant pillow. The hood of her sweatshirt is covering her face. It's only evident it's a girl by the delicate arm resting on her chest and the long, brown hair spilling out underneath her sweatshirt in a messy braid.

"That's just sad," Miles says and walks closer to her. He tentatively pokes the side of her leg with his toe, but she just snorts. "She must be strung out."

"Maybe she's a runaway," I say because she looks young.

"I'm calling the police," Todd says.

"Wait," I say and grab Todd's wrist. My eyes widen with shock when I notice familiar silver rings on her fingers. I bend down to get a closer look at this skinny rail of a girl.

It couldn't be. I inch closer to her and lift the sweatshirt hood. When I see her face I freeze. Long eye lashes, golden freckles, and perfect lips greet me, a face branded in my memory.

"Dylan," I say under my breath. The guys hear me and start to crack up.

"That's Dylan?" Bubba says with disbelief. I slowly nod and keep my eyes focused on her. "That's the chick no one else can compare to, the one you've been pining over all year?"

I stand up and frown. "I haven't been pining," I argue.

"What's wrong with her?" Todd asks with concern in his voice, like she just broke out of a drug rehab clinic.

"Nothing's wrong with her. She's been backpacking through Europe," I inform them. "She probably just got home."

"And came to Albuquerque of all places? I'm not buying it. I bet she hitchhiked here," Bubba says. He walks inside, laughing, and Todd shakes his head and follows him. I cross my arms over my chest and stare down at her. Her mouth is parted slightly and her stomach is rising and sinking in a repetitive motion. I can hear deep breaths move in and out of her nose. She's out cold. Miles stands next to me and studies her.

"So, this is the love of your life?" he asks.

"Was," I remind him. Miles backs up towards the door, either to give me space to pick her up, or out of fear of what will happen when I rouse sleeping beauty.

I study her long, lanky body and frown at those baggy jeans, a style choice she obviously hasn't grown out of. Or into. I say her name a few times to wake her, but all she answers me with is a grumpy moan and I think I hear something like *merci*.

I take a deep breath and scoop her up in my arms. Her comatose body has all the grace of a wet noodle and her arms and legs flop lifelessly as I lift her off the ground. It isn't sexy, but I consider that a good thing. I don't want to see Dylan as sexy. I don't want to see Dylan, period.

Miles opens the door for me and my newly acquired baggage. I carry her up the four flights of stairs to my bedroom. I imagined our reunion several times but in my daydream she always showed up to surprise me naked, or maybe wearing black lingerie. I never imagined it like this, with her mouth hanging open and a strand of drool wetting my T-shirt, just below my collarbone.

I set her down on the bed and she flops over onto her side. A few strands of loose hair stick to the side of her face and neck and I wipe them away. My fingers burn a little at the contact because I forgot how warm and smooth her skin feels. I can remember how sweet it tastes. My eyes linger on her lips, lips that I've spent days, months obsessing over. I have to force myself to look away.

I take her blue, faded tennis shoes off and my nose wrinkles up from the odor that escapes, but I've smelled worse. I consider burning these pathetic shoes, with a frayed hole in the toe and the soles worn almost completely down to the fabric. Yet, knowing her, she's too sentimental to carelessly burn anything. She probably wants to give them a funeral to commemorate their travels together. I set them on my balcony to air out.

I peel off her sweaty socks and frown at the brown stains on the heels. I glance down at her and wonder if she ever did laundry. I contemplate checking her hair for lice. I throw her socks in the trash and notice her jeans are scrunched up around her knees so I decide to slide them off, so she can be comfortable. Or maybe I want to torture myself. I'm relieved her pink underpants look clean. I have to resist letting my fingers run down her legs, legs that I've tasted every inch of, and I cover her with a blanket before I lose any self-control.

I head back downstairs, grab her bag from the porch and pour a glass of water from the sink. When I walk back in my bedroom I can't help but feel like its brighter, like the light has shifted in the sky and more rays are filtering in, but I know why it feels warmer. She always had that effect on my life. I throw her jeans on top of her bag and set the water on the nightstand next to the bed. I stare down at her for a few seconds. I could watch her sleep for the rest of the night and wait for all the old feelings to flood through my heart. But I built a dam to catch those feelings. Well, at least to slow their progress. I grab some shorts to sleep in and escape downstairs before the memories have a chance to catch me.

***

The next morning, I walk into my bedroom to get a change of clothes and try to ignore the energy of a girl whose presence I can feel like a gust of wind, like a storm blowing in. I glance quickly at the bed and Dylan's still sound asleep, rolled up into a ball, her nose and forehead peeking out from under the blanket. I need her out of my room before her presence contaminates everything.

I grab a gray hooded sweatshirt from the top shelf of my closet and I hear her body shift on the mattress as I pull it over my head. Yanking it down over my waist, I turn to see her eyes open now, blinking at the ceiling. I shut the closet door and she turns and squints until her eyes adjust and focus on me. We stare at each other for a few seconds. The room feels too small, as if the walls are slowly compressing around me.

I tell myself I'm not impressed with those huge eyes, eyes that could level me with a single glance. She blinks at me unbelieving, like she's still in a dream. She glances around my room.

"Gray? Where am I?" Her low voice is slower and groggier than normal.

In a mental hospital, I want to say, but she looks too tired for sarcasm.

"In my bedroom," I say. "I thought you might prefer it to the front porch." I pull a UNM baseball cap low over my head. She sits up and the blanket falls to her waist. She rubs her eyes and runs her fingers over her messy heap of bed hair. I try to dwell on the fact that her face is puffy and she has dark circles under her hazel eyes and that I am by no means attracted to her.

My mind quickly shifts to Kari, the girl I met at the Velvet Room last week, in those high boots that walk around in my mind. We've been texting and have plans to hang out next week. I try to focus on that, instead.

"How long have I been asleep?" she asks with a yawn. I tell her about fourteen hours.

"It's Friday morning," I say. Her eyes widen at this.

"I don't think I've slept that long since I was—" and she stops to consider this, resting a finger on her chin.

"In the womb?" I offer and she grins. Her eyes light up when she smiles. It's annoying. She presses a hand against her temple like she's in pain and I point to the glass of water on the nightstand.

"Thanks," she says. She takes a sip and grimaces. I sit down at my desk chair, the furthest spot away from her in the room, the safest spot, and watch her come back to life.

"Do you have anything stronger?" she asks.

I raise an eyebrow. "You want stronger water? Are you used to something lead-based?"

She takes another drink and shakes her head. Yep, too early for sarcasm. "I'm used to coffee as thick as motor oil."

I open my mouth to inform her that this isn't a fricking hotel, but when she pulls her covers off to reveal her bare legs and pink panties, I lose track of thought. She throws me a questioning glance and I divert my eyes and try to look indifferent, like her body has no effect on me. I point out her jeans are on her duffle bag.

She blushes and the color reaches all the way to her lips and my eyes are drawn to them for a second. She lifts her nose and sniffs the air.

"Where are Heidi and Klaus?" she asks.

I stare at her. "Who?"

"My tennis shoes," she says simply, like I should know.

I roll my eyes. She's obviously as random as ever and for some reason this knowledge irritates me. Maybe I was hoping Dylan would change. Grow up. Mellow out. Her unpredictable mind is what I love most about her and if she could suddenly turn boring, it would really help me get over her.

I tell her they're airing out on the balcony and I suggest that she pack a shoe deodorizer the next time she travels. Then, as if I care, she tells me she bought her shoes in Munich and that they've been her best friends these past few months.

"They didn't give me a single blister," she says triumphantly and wriggles her long, pink toes in my direction to prove it. I stare at her naked feet dancing in the air in front of me and something pulls on my heart but I pull back.

She swings her legs over the side of the bed and smiles into my eyes like we're best friends. She starts to explain the history of her shoes, how they're named after this wonderful German couple she met who gave her directions when she was lost—

I stand up and interrupt her because this is getting ridiculous.

"Dylan, I don't care about your shoes. That's not the most pressing issue right now." She blinks back at me and waits.

"What are you doing here?" I say, louder than necessary. Her grin is gone. The sparkle in her eyes fades. She looks disappointed to see anger, not happiness in my eyes. What did she honestly expect? She looks down at her hands and thinks about my question. A few seconds go by.

"I wanted to see you," she says simply. But it isn't simple, I want to tell her. I fold my arms over my chest and hit her with a hard stare.

"It's been over four months," I point out.

"All the more reason to pay you a visit," she says, like I should be happy, like I should be skipping and cart-wheeling and welcoming her with open arms and daisies and a tandem bike ride into the sunset because she finally got around to fitting me back into the travel plan she calls life.

"You're not thinking of staying here, are you?" I ask. It's more of a threat than a question. I thought I was over her. But it's easy to convince yourself you're over someone when they're five thousand miles away. You eventually forget the way they smell, the way their skin tastes and the sound of their voice. Until they show up one day, and, just by looking in their eyes you spiral right back to the place where you started.

She stands up, no longer shy that she's only in a T-shirt and underwear. She takes a few steps towards me and I have to mentally pretend she's my cousin to keep my eyes from falling to her naked legs. She registers the angry look on my face.

"I'll do whatever I want," she says. "Unless I've missed some breaking news story, this is still a free country." She pushes past me and grabs her jeans. I glare down at her, annoyed that *she's* annoyed. She has no right.

"You can't just show up and expect to stay with me," I say. "I have roommates." And a date with a really hot girl, I'm tempted to add. Who wears clean clothes. And showers regularly.

Dylan turns and frowns at me. "I never expected to stay with you," she says as she tugs her jeans on. "I was just taking a power nap." She stumbles as her foot catches in the jeans and I grab her elbow to steady her. My fingers bristle from the contact of her skin and I drop her arm.

I give her the same intense stare I give my catcher when I'm reading the plays.

"Well, my life's a little busy right now," I say. "Some people actually have a routine. I have baseball and classes. You can't just expect me to drop everything and entertain you."

She ignores me and digs around in her duffle bag. I glare down at her. Shouldn't she be apologizing? Begging me to forgive her for so easily crossing me out of her life? She stands up and her face is too close to mine. I take a step back. She doesn't say anything for a few seconds, like she's trying to calculate something in my expression.

"I'm sorry. I just wanted to surprise you," she says.

This makes me laugh, but it sounds forced, rubbed with bitterness.

"What really surprises me Dylan, is that I haven't heard from you in four months," I say as she throws my bedroom door open and drags the duffel bag behind her. She marches down the stairs and shakes her head. Her bag thumps loudly behind her and she shouts over it.

"*You* could have tried to contact *me*," she argues.

"Says the girl with no telephone or permanent address," I yell back. "Is it that hard for *you* to use the phone once in a while?"

She turns to me when she reaches the bottom of the staircase. "I don't understand international calling cards. Too many numbers. It freaks me out."

"What about emailing?" I say and walk down the stairs. "Or do they not have computers in Europe?"

"You never emailed me. At least I sent you postcards," she points out.

"Oh, wow, two postcards, one from Germany telling me 'how many great wieners they have.' Very considerate."

She blinks up at me. "They have amazing hot dogs," she says. "I thought you'd appreciate that."

"That's your idea of keeping in touch?" I ask and lean closer to her.

"I wanted to *surprise* you," she says again, leaning back at me so her face is inches from mine. "But I didn't know your events calendar is completely booked this spring."

I hear a chuckle and wince to see all my roommates sitting in the living room watching us like we're a new reality show, *The Ex-Files*. They all stare at Dylan and she has the nerve to smile and start introducing herself. They're all plenty eager to meet her but I cut them off.

"Don't bother making introductions," I tell Dylan. "You're not staying."

"Do you mind? I'd like to make a good first impression."

"It's a little late," I point out. "They already met you on the front porch when you looked like you were strung out on heroin."

"You say that like it's such a bad thing."

I hear another chuckle and turn to glare but I can't tell who laughed. Dylan's feet stomp along the hardwood floors.

"What about your shoes?"

"I told you. Their names are Heidi and Klaus—"

"I'm not calling them by their names—"

She's out the front door before I can finish. I quickly glance at Bubba as he shakes his head.

"This completely redefines the term sexual tension," he says.

"Stay out of this," I yell back. I slam the front door behind me and follow Dylan onto the grass in the front yard. She unzips a side pocket of her bag and pulls out some silver flip-flops. She kicks her feet into them.

"Where are you going?" I ask.

"I'll figure something out."

I cross my arms over my chest. "Do you have any money?"

"I have seventy-five Euros," she informs me like this currency will work in the U.S.

She bends over and her shirt rides up to expose her bony spine. She lifts her duffel bag with a groan and swings it over her side to use the straps like a backpack. The change in weight takes her body by surprise and she starts to wobble. I take a step towards her.

"Whaa—" she yells as she stammers to the side. I try to grab her but the bag wins and she flies sideways and pulls me down with her onto the grass. She lands half on her bag and half on my chest and our bodies connect with the grass in a muffled thud. We lay there for a moment and despite all my efforts to be mad, I'm cracking up.

"Ow," Dylan moans, her voice close to my ear, her body pressed against mine. She starts laughing and pretty soon we're both laughing so hard my whole body is shaking and I can feel her stomach muscles flexing against mine. I look up and see the sun flooding down on us through tree branches just beginning to bud. I haven't laughed this hard in months. It makes my face hurt.

"That was a graceful exit," Dylan says.

"You're insane," I say through gasps for air.

She pushes herself off my chest and sits up. She slips her arms out of the straps and I lean on my elbows and look in her eyes, eyes that I've smiled and laughed into so many times. It's too easy, too familiar to back here. But I force the thoughts out of my head. I wind them up, stuff them in a ball and smack them into the sky.

She looks away from me and picks at a tuft of grass between us.

"Would it be too much to ask to use your shower?" she asks.

Dylan

Well, that was adequately mortifying. It's not exactly how I imagined our reunion would go. I didn't expect a welcome parade, but a friendly hello would have been appreciated. Instead, I get demoted to not only an unanticipated visitor, but an *unwanted* one. Harsh. And Gray has no idea how flushed he gets when he's mad and how it just makes his eyes blaze and his cheeks blush and how our entire, stupid fight just felt like foreplay.

Catherine was right. I didn't want to really believe it, but I see it now. Gray needed more from me. I realize how much I've let him down.

Now I'm naked in his shower, which is awkward because it's just making me picture him naked. The water doesn't help me relax. It pelts my skin, like it's angry, like it's pushing me to hurry up and get out. Or, maybe I'm just not used to really good water pressure.

I dry off and wrap a faded yellow towel around my chest. I wipe the steam off the bathroom mirror, meeting eyes that are still puffy and skin that's dry and peeling around my nose. I dab some lotion on my face, brush my teeth, and contemplate where I went wrong, and more importantly, how to make this up to Gray.

Maybe I've watched movies like *The Cutting Edge* and *When Harry Met Sally* and *A lot Like Love* and *Ever After* and *While You Were Sleeping* and *Say Anything* (just to name a

few) one too many times. Is my hopelessly romantic idea
of love just an unrealistic collection of Hollywood movie
clips? Have I convinced myself that my love life could
mirror the high-intensity story plots of fictional characters?

I guess I did. Huh.

But what is life without love? It's what inspires us,
what drives us, what keeps our bodies warm on cold nights
and our hearts soft when they want to harden with
loneliness. So why hold it back? Then, the worst thought
of all strikes: Gray doesn't love me anymore.

I stare at my reflection and see the disbelief on my
face. Is it possible to fall in and out of love, like it's just a
season, just a trend? Can love be an illusion—a moment
that passes—like any other fleeting emotion?

I pull on the khaki pants Catherine's grandmother
gave me. They're too short and hang low off my waist, but
they're the cleanest ones I have. I throw on my jean jacket
and check out my appearance in the full-length mirror. Not
exactly stunning.

I make a mental note: *In the future, do not attempt to win a
boy's heart when you look like you were just released from a refugee
camp.* I lift my chin and try to shake off my doubts. All I
can do is be myself.

I spring down the stairs and through the front door to
find Gray sitting on the steps in the sun waiting for me.
His elbows are resting on his knees and he's staring out at
the street. I sit down next to him and run a comb through
damp hair that smells like his shampoo, like musk or spice
or something.

He leans away from me, a little stiffly.

"You know," I say, "I've always wondered why men
and women's shampoos smell so different. Why do guys
want to smell like Ocean Mist and Steel Ice? And how is
Steel Ice even a scent? And who decided women prefer to

smell like fruits baskets?" I wait for him to help explain my observation, but he studies me without a trace of a grin.

"I'm not really in the mood for your random questions right now," he says. I stare back at him and wrinkle my eyebrows. I had considered it a very serious question.

"You must be hungry," he says in a flat voice. I pat my empty stomach and swear it feels concave. I nod and start to tell him the bar of soap in the shower looked like a block of cheddar cheese, but then I remember his comment and bite my lips together.

"I'm low on groceries," he says. "But there's a café down the street." He stands up and frowns when he takes in my outfit.

"Seriously, Dylan?"

I set the comb down on the porch step. "What?" I ask.

"You're the only girl I've ever met that goes out of her way to dress *badly*."

"It's okay," I say and tug on the collar of my jacket. "It's vintage." I open up the front of the coat to show Gray the inside lining and he shudders at the sight of the striped flannel. His reaction makes me laugh. I pick myself up and stick my hip out to the side like I'm posing for a magazine cover.

"Hey, this style is the rage in Europe right now," I say.

Gray studies his fingernails. "I'm sure."

He turns and heads for the sidewalk and I fall into step next to him. "It's not my fault this country's lagging behind in fashion."

"It must be hard being a trendsetter," Gray says, keeping his eyes straight ahead.

"It's a huge responsibility," I agree. "Fashion is a risk. I pull it off with a balance of confidence, mystique and rebellion."

Gray shakes his head and his lip twitches at one corner. It isn't even close to a smile, but it's a start. I sneak looks at his profile while we walk. His thick, shaggy dark hair spills out from under his hat, his blue eyes mirror the sky, and he's tan and even more gorgeous than I remembered. I glance down at his long fingers with veins wrapped around the knuckles—the sexiest hands in the world. I remember things his hands have done to me and my face flushes. Meanwhile, his face has all the emotional investment of a rock.

Gray informs me the team's leaving this afternoon to go on the road until Sunday. My heart sinks at the news. I have to wait three more days to talk to him? I haven't seen him for months and my stealth reentrance into his life has consisted of passing out like a drunk, sleeping for twenty hours like a bum, and then making a scene in front of his roommates worthy of a Most Dramatic Female award.

"You can crash at my place if you need to," he offers, but his voice is still hostile.

No way.

I shake my head. "No, thanks," I say.

He regards me with blue eyes that are darker, stormier than normal. A shadow slides over them every time he looks at me. "You have other options?" he asks.

"I might."

"Who else do you know in Albuquerque?"

"Catherine," I say.

"Catherine, who?"

I stall because I'm terrible at remembering names. "Catherine, um, Catherine Kra-ker-krin-skin," I stammer. He's frowning, which means he knows I'm clueless.

"Catherine Krakerkrinskin?" he mocks.

I laugh and admit I don't know her last name. I tell him I met her in Interlaken. He just stares at me like I mentioned a planet in the Triangulum Galaxy.

"Where's that?"

"Switzerland," I say. I explain she plays for a band here, named Charlie's Angels or Angels in Charge or—

"Chuck's Angel?" he asks. He stops halfway up the steps in front of the café and stares at me. "You met Cat Parker in Switzerland?"

"Parker," I say. "I was close." He rolls his eyes and we stand on the steps in the sun while I perform a dramatic retelling of the evening I lost my luggage and was stranded and saved all within the same hour. He shakes his head and opens the door to the café. We're met with a buzz of commotion. I glance around to see an entire restaurant full of college students studying, or pretending to study, but mostly talking on cell phones or to each other. I watch girls checking out Gray, whispering and smiling and laughing like they're all in on a secret. I glance at Gray to see if he notices the attention, but he's watching me with a frown.

"What?" I ask.

"You're like Forest Gump," he says while we wait in line. "Everything works out for you. You always meet the right people at the right time and it's all an accident."

"Maybe it's not an accident at all," I say and study a long chalkboard suspended on hooks over the cash registers. "But I always love a good Tom Hanks movie reference." I smile at him but he won't meet my eyes. I look back at the menu, written out in small, block letters. I lick my lips and feel my stomach buckle from hunger pains.

"I can loan you some money," Gray offers. I stick my nose up in the air and shake my head because the last thing I want from him is a handout. All I want are his lips and his mind and his body. I decline to mention this.

"I have money," I say. I hope. I dig into the front pocket of my jeans and pull out a crumpled wad of cash. I separate the Euros from a few dollar bills.

I squint up at the prices listed on the blackboard—I'm determined not to go over my $3.75. Gray starts talking to a girl behind the cash register and I try to make my mind up but even the condiments on the counter look appetizing. I start to salivate at the ketchup and mustard dispensers. I haven't had ketchup in months. I reach over and pump a dab of red sauce on my finger and suck it off slowly to enjoy the sweet tomato flavor.

"Mmm, that's so good," I say to no one in particular. I reach my finger out to taste the mustard, but Gray grabs my wrist.

"It's not an appetizer," he informs me.

"Hey, want to know the most bizarre food item I've ever seen on a menu?" I ask him.

He raises his eyebrows.

"Bull testicles. Isn't that sick? It's considered a delicacy."

"Where? In prison?" he asks.

"In Montana, I think. They're called Rocky Mountain Oysters and—"

"Would you just order?" Gray barks.

I face forward obediently, like a kid reprimanded by an impatient parent. The girl behind the counter narrows her eyes at me, but it's more out of curiosity than annoyance.

She's wearing a Brew House T-shirt, the front featuring a yellow outline of a coffee mug with steam curling above the cup. Over the T-shirt she's wearing a bright orange apron that looks like a tattoo artist practiced patterns using a black magic marker. There are swirling snakes and daggers and dragons and skulls and crossbones all over it. The images are angry and morbid and I sense an "I hate my life," vibe radiating off her. There's even an illustration of a python strangling a coffee mug. I meet her eyes and smile. Her outfit makes an obvious statement.

"Great apron," I tell her. "I get the feeling this isn't your dream job?" She yanks on her lip ring and glances at Gray.

"I think that's the first thing you said to me," she tells him.

I order a sandwich and set my money on the counter. I notice this girl glance at me and back at Gray and Gray looks at me and back at her like we're playing stare tag. I decide to call them out on their little game.

"Listen," I say. "If I have toothpaste stuck to my face, would one of you just point it out instead of gawking at me?"

"You must be Dylan," she says. I nod and she extends her small hand to shake mine. "I'm Lenny," she says. "It's an honor."

Gray

Take a deep breath. Okay, so the ghost of love's past just paid you a surprise visit. No reason to freak out.

I slam my hands into the pocket of my hooded sweatshirt and stomp to class. I avoid eye contact. Usually every other person I pass recognizes me on campus, but I can't muster up a fake smile right now. Not when my chest is smoking. I pull the rim of my cap down low and turn my music up.

My lips flatten into a tight line. This is not happening. She is *not* staying.

Dylan's a smart girl. She definitely got the hint that I'm not exactly thrilled to see her. She might even be gone before I get back on Sunday and that would be for the best. Besides, what do we have to say to each other? Neither of us does small talk, and why rehash old memories that are better swept under the rug?

We can't recreate what we had. You can't bring back the past. So why fight about it?

Also, I'm obviously not attracted to her. I take a deep sigh of relief as this fact resonates through my mind, like cold ice soothing a burn. What did I ever see in her? She's skinnier than I remembered. She almost looks malnourished. I like curves. And that wild hair—is she ever going to cut it? Her clothes—seriously, she's too old to dress like a bum. It was interesting in Phoenix because it was different, but now it's just embarrassing. People know me on campus. I can't be seen with a girl who looks like I picked her up from the local soup kitchen. People are going to assume I'm doing community service, not hanging out with my girlfriend.

I have an image to maintain.

But she smelled really good in my shampoo and her eyes still make the energy in the room shift. Her smile still heats the air and my mind and makes something hollow feel occupied by something warm.

But that's just because we've been intimate. Some feelings are bound to resurface. That's normal. We've had sex. We've had sex multiple, okay, maybe hundreds of times. And it was toe-curling, mind-blowing—

No, no, it wasn't that good. Not with Dylan. It couldn't have been. She's not even my type. She's just this novel creature, this rare specimen. And when it comes to sex, I just have nothing else to compare it to. I need a second opinion, that's all. I need to get laid.

That's it. Maybe I'll hit it off with Kari. Kari lives here, she's in college, I can relate to her. Dylan's just a girl in my past. She lives in a playground of her imagination and that's the last thing I need right now.

But then why is everything so effortless with her? Why is it so easy to want the wrong person?

Dylan

Relax and breathe. Okay, things didn't go quite the way
you hoped. Scratch that. Things didn't go even a fraction
of a decimal point close to the way you hoped, but no need
to panic. Count your blessings. You have your health and
your wisdom and all your teeth.

I sit on my duffel bag on the top of Gray's balcony
and stare out at the rooftops stretching below. I've never
felt more lost, like a feather plucked out of a bird that
slowly descends to the ground only to look misplaced.
Where do I go from here?

At least I didn't go out of my way to tie a big red bow
around my naked body. That would have been sufficiently
humiliating. Gray might have used it to hang me from the
nearest tree. That's about how happy he was to see me.

All I want is for Gray to love me. And he not only
doesn't love me, he downright loathes me. He mega
loathes me. It's so strange that people get angry, not by
what you do, but by what you *don't* do.

I look at the rooftops huddled around me and I want
to skip across them and slide down a chimney chute into a
place I feel welcome. Right now I feel like an intruder. I
want Dick Van Dyke to pop out of a chimney and sing,
"Step in Time," and then draw a chalk picture of a perfect
landscape for me to jump into. Why can't I just add a

spoon full of sugar to sweeten the sad moments in life? Why don't birds land on my finger when I whistle to them? I keep trying, but it never works for me.

I need to move, but what direction do I take? I didn't plan one step ahead of this moment. I have a summer job waiting for me in Wisconsin, but not until June. I have almost three months to kill and no money. This is what I get for following my heart—a big dose of rejection.

I make a mental note: *Next time you take directions from your heart, plan on getting lost.*

I count my net worth, and once I convert it to dollars, I'll have about $100. I stare into the horizon and contemplate how to spend it. If I'm lucky, it will just be enough to cover a bus ride back to Wisconsin. And then what? I'll be stuck living with my parents and getting a job with all my high school townie friends whose idea of traveling is ice fishing up north. Everyone will say "I told you so" and "look where you end up when you don't plan better." Broke. Living under your parents' roof. Suckling the parental teat.

My future becomes terrifyingly clear. I'm forty years old, still living at home in a room above the garage. My wardrobe consists of a plaid bathrobe and white orthopedic slippers. I don't bother shaving my legs anymore. My skin smells like Lubriderm lotion and my robe smells like cranberry potpourri air freshener. I raid my parent's refrigerator everyday for leftovers because all I have in my place is a hot pad and a mini fridge. I spend every night reading trashy romance novels with my four cats curled around my feet: Fiffi, Fluffy, FooFoo and Fro.

Ugh. The image is too painful to endure.

I shake my head to break free of this nightmare. I stand up, suck in a deep breath, and make a decision I'm determined to keep. I'm going to stay in Albuquerque. I'm going to show Gray he can depend on me. I'm going to prove that even if there's distance, even if our relationship isn't perfectly spread out before us like a map from point A to point B, it doesn't mean it's over. Maybe our relationship curves and dips and weaves and cuts off and forks and then comes together again, but maybe that's who we are and who we need to be. Besides, aren't the things you work the hardest for, the sweetest victory in the end?

I am not giving up on Gray. It isn't over between us.

Feeling better, I pull out a piece of paper with Catherine's address and email written on it and I pray she'll be a little more excited to see me.

***

A half hour later I find Sage Street. It's unnerving to discover Cat lives about six blocks away from Gray's house. It's one of my stranger fates. I hear someone strumming a guitar and I follow the sound until Cat's in view, sitting on a brown couch on the front porch of a small, single story green house tucked between two maple trees. I swing my duffel bag down on the ground to find my camera. I take a couple shots of Cat while she's stuck inside a creative haze before she notices me. She stops strumming and blinks over at me.

"Dylan?" she asks, though she doesn't look surprised to see me. She already knows me too well. "What are you doing here?"

I set my camera down and laugh at myself. At this point, it's either laugh or cry my eyes out.

"I took your advice," I say as I walk through the grass to the porch steps. She stands up and sets her guitar on the couch. "I came back to see Gray."

She regards my face. "It didn't go too well?"

I sit down on the steps and shake my head. There's an ivy plant crawling up the metal railing and I rub the smooth leaves between my fingers. Cat walks over and sits down next to me.

"It appears time has two different effects on the heart," I say, still looking at the leaves. "It either makes it swell with love or shrivel with bitterness."

"Yeah," Cat agrees. "It's usually one extreme or the other."

I nod and a long sigh escapes my chest. She wraps her arm around me and I rest my head on her warm, soft shoulder.

"The good thing is," Cat says, "the heart has an amazing capacity to forgive. It might just take a little convincing."

We sit out on the porch for a few minutes. Cat rubs my arm and I think about forgiveness and try to walk around in Gray's shoes. I try to understand exactly what I did wrong.

Cat tells me she has a place I can crash. She grabs my duffel bag and I follow her to a one-car garage detached from the house. She unlocks the door and explains she used to use the space for band practice, but they've been signing so many shows they hardly need it anymore. I look around at the renovated apartment. There are huge windows along one wall that faces out to a row of tall sycamore trees. There's a small bathroom attached to it, and a futon with a pile of blankets folded on top. The floor is gray cement with a few woven rugs scattered around the space. The walls are painted light brown, and a few apple crates piled on top of each other form a makeshift shelf, stuffed full of music books. I set my bag down next to it.

"It's perfect," I say. I promise Cat I'm going to look for a temporary job and I'll pay her rent as soon as I can.

"How long do you think you'll stay?" she asks as she helps me sort through my heap of dirty clothes.

I shrug. *Until Gray forgives me.* "I have a summer job back in Wisconsin, so maybe a few months, if it's okay," I tell her. I hope it's enough time.

Gray

Sunday night the team bus pulls into the parking lot of the Lobo center after a three game weekend. We're all sunburned, exhausted, and starving. Why didn't I get groceries before I left town? Oh, yeah, because I had some unexpected company.

After we separate our gear, we pack into Todd's car and Travis joins us because he lives next door with a couple football players. We all discuss ordering pizza.

"I'm broke," Bubba says.

"You say that every time we order out," Miles says.

"Well, every time I'm broke."

"Maybe if you stopped spending all your money on Amy…," Travis hints.

"We broke up, but thanks for mentioning it," Bubba says.

When we pull into the driveway, Todd slows down and stares up at the house. Half the lights downstairs are turned on. Bubba turns and glares at me.

"Dude, did you give that crazy girl keys to our house?" he asks.

"What crazy girl?" Travis asks.

I shake my head and insist she's staying with a friend.

"Then who gets the numbskull award for leaving the lights on?" Bubba asks.

We grab our bags out of the trunk and I'm the first one to the house. The front door's unlocked, and when I walk inside, I'm hit with smells that make my mouth water—garlic, butter and marinara sauce.

I hear footsteps and Dylan appears in the hallway. She's wearing a green apron around her signature baggy shirt and jeans. Her hair is braided in pigtails.

"Welcome home!" she says. The other guys walk in and drop their bags.

"What is that glorious smell?" Bubba asks.

"Dinner," Dylan says as she wipes some flour off her arm. "I hope you're not mad," she says, her eyes directed at me.

"How did you get in?" I ask.

"You left your bedroom door unlocked."

I narrow my eyes. "So unlawful entry is justified if it comes with a home cooked meal?" I ask her. I frown at her smile, her thoughtful gesture, her appearance in general. "Since when do you cook?" I ask.

"Ha," she says. "Me? Cook? That's just a fire hazard."

Before I can respond, out walks Lenny, holding a steaming pot of lasagna in hands covered with red oven mitts. I didn't even know we owned oven mitts.

"Dinner's ready," Lenny says.

The guys pass us to get to the kitchen, shoving each other like little kids running to get to the front of the lunch line. I notice Travis give Dylan a double take. I watch her closely and I don't know if I should be happy she's here, or angry. But I'm not surprised. She turns and heads back to the kitchen with her bouncy gait.

I drop my bag and follow her, annoyed that something has so naturally shifted. In the room. Inside of me.

***

Dinner is amazing—homemade garlic bread and lasagna. They found enough extra chairs in our basement so we could have a meal around the table. Dylan folded napkins under our mismatched silverware. She lit two candles on the table for ambiance. She claims she found the candles in the kitchen cupboard but none of the guys will fess up to owning them.

"This was fantastic, Lenny," Miles says and she tries to hide her pride in the fact that five ravenous guys have inhaled every scrap of food on the table.

Bubba pats his full stomach and asks Lenny to marry him. I catch Lenny blush. She's always had a thing for Native American guys. It never occurred to me that Bubba is completely her type. I also notice Travis's eyes scanning Dylan's face one too many times. But he couldn't be attracted to her. She's a mess, with her hair falling out of her pigtails and she's still wearing that stupid apron.

Dylan wants to talk about the game, but she doesn't ask the score or how many base hits we had, all the normal questions you'd expect. She wants to know why the dugout is called the dugout, and what we think while we're running the bases, and if we could play for any pro team who would it be, and what exactly is a Lobo, and if we couldn't play baseball again, ever, what would we do with our lives?

I just listen because this is the Dylan I missed. I spend most of the meal watching her eyes absorb every face around her, and watching her mind absorb every word. She's so good at being right there, in the moment.

I look around the room at all these eyes on her and realize there's safety in numbers. Maybe I can handle having Dylan back in my life if I keep it to big groups. I just have to avoid being alone with her. That's when I feel the force of her energy seep through my skin. That's when she plants herself deep in my veins, like she's part of my blood stream. When her energy is widely dispersed, like right now, it doesn't trap me.

This is my new survival plan.

Travis leans forward and gives Dylan his full attention. He focuses his green eyes on hers, hitting her with a gaze I've seen girls fall to mush under. I've heard girls nickname him the Best Catch, not only because he's our catcher, but because he's 6'2" and single. I have to admit it, he's an amazing player. He can cover any position in a pinch. Even though he's tall, he can run the bases as well as the sprinters. He has the most home runs of the season. He's more than aware of his skills, so he's awarded himself a reputation equivalent to God.

"What do you do?" Travis asks Dylan in a tone that is more interrogating than friendly. I glance at Dylan but she isn't intimidated.

"Lately, I'm a full-time star doodler," she says.

"A what?" he asks.

"I draw stars on everything. It's this weird habit." She flips her hand over to show she's drawn a few stars on her palm.

Travis tries a different question. "Do you live here?" he asks.

"No," I chime in. I know Dylan well enough to predict that her eccentric answers could go on all night and I'm not in the mood. Travis, Dylan, and the entire table turn to look at me. I set my glass of iced tea on the table with a loud thud.

"She's just passing through town," I say. Her eyes meet mine for a second and they narrow.

"Are you in school?" Travis asks.

"It depends what you consider school," Dylan says. "I believe in self-directed education. It's this new, hands-on approach to learning."

Travis looks at me with exasperation. "What the hell is she talking about?"

I raise one of my shoulders. Their conversation reminds me of the way I first reacted when I met Dylan, the way you react to something you've never come across before. You question and poke and pry to try and understand it. Or you run from it.

"Water down the crazy talk, Dylan," I say to her. "You're scaring my friends."

"I'm not going to college," she says to Travis. "I think as long as you have goals and you're striving for them, that's all that matters. It's not what you learn in school, it's what you do in life that teaches you the most."

There's a few seconds of silence as the table tries to grasp what she's saying.

"Okay, so what are your goals?" Bubba asks.

"Well, first and foremost I want to travel the world. I also want to learn how to play an instrument, like the harmonica or maybe the mouth harp. I'd like to job shadow a volcanologist, or maybe train to be a hot air balloon pilot."

I watch the table studying her with expressions ranging between confused and amused.

"Is she serious?" Travis asks me and I just shrug my shoulders.

"Then I have daily goals," she continues. "I try and accomplish one new thing a day."

"Like?" Miles asks.

"Today I roasted a marshmallow over a candle."

"That was your goal for today?" Travis asks her.

Dylan nods like it's a perfectly respectable goal. "It takes a lot of patience and just the right flame proximity to avoid burning the marshmallow. It's a practiced skill."

"This is true," Lenny said. "I witnessed it."

I watch Lenny and she's smiling. I can tell she has fallen for Dylan, which annoys me. Lenny doesn't like me half the time and I'm one of her best friends. Come to think of it, I'm one of her only friends. This confirms my theory. Give Dylan time and she can win over anybody.

Except for me. I know better than to fall under her spell. I know the end result.

Bubba asks Dylan what she plans to do while she's out here. I sit back in my chair and study her. I've been wondering the same thing.

"I can hire you part time at the cafe," Lenny offers and I shoot her a warning glare.

"I'm a terrible waitress," Dylan admits. She taps the side of her head with her finger. "No short term memory."

Todd mentions his girlfriend works at a clothes boutique and he can ask her if they're hiring. I almost laugh out loud at this. The thought of Dylan selling clothes is as absurd as someone in a wheelchair selling running shoes. She's fashion handicapped.

"It must be kind of slim pickings without a college degree," Travis comments. His voice is condescending, but Dylan just grins back. The more I get to know Travis, the more I see he lives for pushing people until they fire back at him. He likes to fight.

"College isn't for me," she says. She gets this pensive look on her face and I bite my lips together to hide a smile. Here comes her deep thought for the day. "I'm impressed with people who can whittle down what they want to do to one single thing. Don't you think it's strange that our whole lives we're taught how to act and what to think?

Then we graduate from high school and all of a sudden, bam, we're supposed to know exactly who we are and what we want to do, even though we were never given a chance to figure it out. It doesn't make sense to me."

"What hippie colony were you raised in?" Bubba asks. Everybody else is just staring at her.

"So, who do you know here?" Travis asks.

Dylan points at me with her fork.

"We met in Phoenix last summer," I say. "She's just a friend."

I feel the table regarding me. Friends. That's one way to put it.

Dylan

After dinner Lenny and Travis take off, but I stay to help clean up. I'm determined to talk to Gray tonight, even though he's equally determined to avoid me, like he's afraid of being alone with me. He and Bubba recap the games while they do dishes and I busy myself with clearing the table and putting away folding chairs. Miles sits down with me and we discuss the differences between cricket and baseball. He's shy, but in this endearing way. I wonder if Cat would like him because he sweet and cute and doesn't seem cocky at all, like she describes athletes.

When the guys are done washing dishes they all head to the living room except for Gray, who disappears. I walk outside to find him sitting in a chair on the porch, staring out at the yard. He stands up when he sees me and regards me with eyes that are careful. Too careful. Like there are walls behind them. We both stand there and wait for the other person to make the first move.

"How are you getting home?" he asks.

"I'm walking."

He sighs through his nose and shakes his head. "Not alone."

"It's only a few blocks," I insist. "Cat lives on Sage Street."

"Come on," he says. "I'm walking you."

The night's cool and there's a chill in the breeze. I want to lean against Gray, I want him to wrap his arm around my shoulders, but instead the cold air bites at my skin and Gray keeps a safe distance. We walk for a few minutes and silence stretches around us. It's so quiet I can hear the electrical hum of the streetlights. I look up and see the North Star shining—the brightest light in the sky. Looking at it gives me inspiration.

"Have you ever heard of a nova?" I ask.

Gray looks up at the sky and shrugs.

"I read about it," I say. "It's a sudden increase in the brightness of a star. It makes a dim, dormant star light up until it's the brightest object in the sky. Everything is ignited until all this energy builds up and it shines."

Gray glares back at me. He knows what I'm getting at. "That's nuclear fusion," he says. "And the star eventually blows up because it can't handle the reaction." He looks away as I picture this depressing image. Leave it to Gray to see the dark side of my love analogy. Guess that tactic didn't work.

"Since we're on an astrological kick," Gray says, "have you heard of an eclipse?" I narrow my eyes because I know where he's going with this. "One second the sun's shining and life is great and then all of a sudden, it disappears," he says. "It just flitters off because it can never sit still."

I stop walking and turn to face Gray, my arms crossed over my chest. He stops walking and stares at me.

"Okay, let's stop playing this little metaphor mind game because unlike most girls, I don't live for drama."

He crosses his arms and stands in the same rigid posture. "Like I do?"

"Gray, I'm sorry I didn't call you when I was in Europe. I'm sorry I didn't give you a heads up when I was coming back. I don't think logically," I remind him, and he rolls his eyes. "I thought when I saw you over Christmas, we agreed we'd see each other when we could make it happen. I should have stayed in touch better, and I know I let you down. I just hope you can forgive me." I decide it's time to throw out the words I've been waiting to say for months.

"I still love you," I tell him.

He frowns at me and I know what he's thinking. He thinks I throw that word around too easily. "A lot's changed."

"Like what?"

"What if I have a girlfriend?"

I stare at him. "Do you?"

"No," he says and I take a breath of relief. "But what if I did?" he argues. I start walking again and he follows me. "What if I'm over you? What if I moved on just like you were pushing me to do the first time you left?"

I fix my eyes on his. "Have you moved on?" I wait to hear the words validated but he doesn't answer me. "Gray, we can play the 'what if' game all night," I say. "I happen to love that game. What if you could breathe underwater? What if a human baby was born with six tongues?"

Gray cocks his head to the side as he considers this one. "That could never happen."

"What if a meteor the size of Texas hits the earth in two hours and sixteen minutes?" I continue. "But what's the point? We can go back and forth all night wondering what if and miss the fact that this is it, this is life happening in front of us right now and we're missing it, dwelling on things that haven't happened."

He shakes his head and I know what's bugging him. "See, you can be logical," he says.

"I know it's been a while, but we've both been busy and happy and living out our dreams. Right?"

His eyes have lost some of their anger and I figure out what's wrong. He isn't happy. The shadows are back. The lack of sleep. I know he's up late. Thinking. Overanalyzing. I know his mind never quiets down and that's one of the greatest things about him. But I can't help that we met when we were so young, just when our lives were peaking with change. I can't help that I wasn't willing to give up my dreams, just when I was starting to live them.

"What's wrong with picking up where we left off?" I ask him. "Why can't we just make the most of the time we have together when we have it? I thought that's what we wanted?"

Gray smirks. "Because from my personal experience, Dylan, falling in love with you is like jumping out of an airplane with no parachute. It's fun as hell, a rush of adrenaline, until the inevitable crash comes where you leave and my heart splatters all over the ground."

"Interesting theory," I mumble. We get to my driveway and Gray looks over at my little apartment, lit softly by a lamp in the window.

"Do you want me to leave town?" I ask.

He takes a deep breath. "I don't know," he says. "I came out here to get a fresh start. This place has no memories attached to my family or my sister or to you. Now you come along, and I know your style. You're going to leave your mark everywhere. And it's all fun and games for you, but you're leaving again. Being the person that gets left behind sucks because I have to live with all the memories. I had to do that with Amanda in Phoenix. I've had to do it with you. I can't do it again. I'm done."

I nod and it surprises me that I've never considered it from his side. It makes me feel selfish, because he's right.

Gray doesn't spread his love out like I do. He saves it for a few worthy people and he allows himself to depend on those people.

"I don't want to be weaved in and out of your life when it's convenient for you. So if you want to stay here, fine, but don't do it for me. We're over." He turns and heads down the street without another word and I watch his shadow grow smaller in the distance.

Gray

Kari and I text back and forth and she sends me messages like "miss you," and "you're cute," and I wonder if she's stealing phrases from a box of valentine heart candy. I ask her out for dinner by text since she prefers to communicate that way, and we swap restaurant ideas. She wants to eat at Harvest, this all-organic five-star gourmet restaurant, and yeah, I'd love to eat there too, if someone else was treating. We agree on Firefly, a local restaurant Todd recommends that's perfect for a date. Girls will respect you for supporting a local business, and you don't break your budget.

On the way to pick up Kari, I stop at the Brew House to loan Lenny my copy of *Super Troopers* and she meets me outside for a cigarette. She observes my combed hair and wrinkle-free shirt.

"What fraternity did you recently join?" she asks me.

"I'm taking Kari out to dinner," I remind her.

She takes a long drag on her cigarette and her eyes turn into attack mode.

"I thought you were above being a player."

I take offense at this. "I'm not being a player. I have a date. I asked Kari out over a week ago."

"So, cancel it," she says.

"Why should I?"

She just shakes her head. "You're wasting your time, Gray. And your money," she informs me. "Stop trying to punish Dylan. You're just punishing yourself."

I laugh at this assumption. "She's been back for less than a week, and I'm supposed to drop everything?"

Lenny exhales a puff of smoke and stares at me like I might be suffering from brain damage. "Don't you get it? She's trying to make it up to you. She's trying to prove you can depend on her. She came back here and you're pushing her away and she's staying and taking it because she loves you."

I shove my hands in my pockets. "We're not getting back together." I say the words like a mantra.

"Get over yourself. She's perfect for you. I've never seen you so entertained by someone—and I've seen you really high," she adds and points a finger at me.

I throw my arms up in the air. "Yeah, isn't she great? She makes everyone fall in love with her. It's her gift. It's her survival plan, so she can travel the world and be a mooch."

Lenny frowns at me. "She's not a mooch. She's the one that paid for all those groceries the other night."

"This is all temporary to her," I argue. "You're all infatuated right now because she's funny and she's different. But you can't depend on her. One day she's going to get bored and leave and cancel you out of her life."

"I don't think that's true. I think you can count on Dylan more than anyone. I like her Gray, and you know me. I barely like you half the time and you're my best friend."

I can feel my shoulders slump when I hear this. Lenny should be taking my side. Now she's suddenly suiting up to join Team Dylan? Traitor.

"I'll admit I still care about Dylan when you admit you have a crush on my roommate," I argue.

She glowers back at me. "What? You're ridiculous."

"You said you'd never date athletes. You're so full of it."

"Bubba's not my type."

"He's completely your type. Not that I'm okay with that. Bubba needs to grow up before he dates you and I don't see him hitting maturity until he's at least forty-seven."

"We're not talking about me. We're talking about you and Dylan."

"No," I say. "We're done talking about Dylan." I toss the movie into Lenny's lap and head towards my car.

"You're being a chicken shit," she yells.

"Thanks for the support," I say over my shoulder. "You're a really terrific friend."

Lenny stubs out her cigarette and stands up. "If you don't start being nice to Dylan, I'll set her up with someone who will."

It's an empty threat but it still pisses me off. "Stay out of this, Lenny!" I say, but before I get in my car I thank her for cooking the amazingly delicious lasagna. She responds by giving me the finger.

***

I pick Kari up at 7:00. She's wearing a skirt that shows off her slim legs and shiny red heels that show off her ankles. Her skin smells like coconut lotion and her dark hair curls loosely around her shoulders.

When we sit down at Firefly, she unbuttons her jacket to reveal a very low cut blouse, a nice view to add to my dining enjoyment. Her lips are thin but she accentuates them with red lipstick and I can't help but wonder what Dylan's lips would look like if she ever bothered to paint them.

No more Dylan comparisons. Kari has curves. Kari combs her hair. Cleans her clothes. Trims her nails instead of biting them off. She's a woman.

We sit down in a booth across from each other. This is already strange. Dylan never sat across from me in a booth. She wanted to be right next to me, touching hands and knees and feet and arms.

Stop it, Gray. Kari. Date. Now. Focus.

I clear my throat and ask her how her classes are going. I'm trying to watch her eyes, but something keeps sparkling when she moves and I realize it's glitter lotion strategically rubbed all over her chest. Great. I feel like I'm back in Phoenix.

Kari says her classes are "oh, you know, okay," and I tell her mine are about the same. She asks me what I'm taking this semester and I list my schedule and she lists hers. I try to swallow a yawn, but it escapes. Small talk is up there with dental cleanings as an entertaining way to pass the time. I sit back in my chair and realize this is the first dinner date I've been on since Dylan, unless you count Lenny, but a taco run at 2 a.m. to satisfy the munchies doesn't really qualify as a date.

The waitress stops and asks if we'd like to order an appetizer. There's this awkward moment where we both gaze over our menus and go through this polite exchange of, 'oh, I like whatever, oh, me too,' so we can't decide on anything.

"We need another minute," I tell the waitress. She walks away and I hint that the calamari sounds good, but Kari squishes her face together and points out that it's deep fried. I say, okay, how about the spinach dip, and she says it's too creamy. Cream based dips are high in fat, she points out, and she might be lactose intolerant. I suggest the nachos and she says they're usually smothered in grease. And cheese. I bite my lips together and go for one more, the coconut shrimp, which I point out is baked, not fried, and zero dairy.

"I'm a vegetarian," she informs me.

I close the menu and take a long drink of water. She can have the bread basket and like it. I hope there aren't too many carbs for her to handle and I hope the oil won't make her skin break out and I hope she's okay with gluten. And she better not drill me on the unfair treatment of cows when I order a tenderloin steak—bloody.

The waitress takes our order and when she leaves Kari sips her iced tea. I slam half my Diet Coke which makes me want to belch but I hold it in which really hurts. I think the worst part about first dates is feeling self-conscious about natural bodily functions. That just sucks. There is nothing more painful than feeling compelled to hold in gas.

I stare across the table at Kari and this heavy silence falls.

She spins a dark lock of hair around her finger and smiles at me. We settle for conversations that feel like I'm filling out a personality questionnaire. What are you majoring in? Where are you from? What kind of food do you like to eat? Have you been to this restaurant before? Really, do you come here often? Isn't the ambiance great? Yeah, it's really great. I prefer sitting in booths don't you? Yeah, booths are great. Do you have any brothers or sisters? This question used to make my stomach curl, but I've gotten used to it. The answer is no. Always no. I'm an only child. Next question.

But when I tell Kari I'm an only child, her mouth drops with pity.

"I'd hate to be an only child," she says. I just smile because when I was little, I used to pray Amanda would get kidnapped so I could live in peace. This usually happened after Amanda stole my G.I. Joe's and I found them hanging out with her Barbies, or when we watched *The Little Mermaid* everyday for a year, and she made me dress as Eric for Halloween so her best friend could be Ariel and then they suckered me into a pretend wedding where I had to kiss her friend. I used to lie in bed at night and pray for a brother (even though the thought of my parents actually having sex scared me more than the thought of being abducted by aliens and used for medical experiments). I wanted brothers to rough house with. I wanted wrestling matches that would put hair on my chest. Guys I knew that grew up with brothers have these great fishing stories. They have scars from all the fights they've been in. I have stories of dressing up in drag when my sister convinced me to play "beauty salon" with her and her friends.

"I've always wanted a sibling," I finally say.

"I think it would be so cool to have a twin," Kari says. She can't help that she's hitting below the belt, but the date is already as fun as a formal job interview so why not throw another awkward log on the fire?

My mind drifts to Dylan. All our moments together were so hilarious. We killed hours in restaurants because we were babbling too much to eat and laughing so hard one of us choked or snorted at least once per meal. We were too busy analyzing the people around us—writing the biography of the cook or the bus boy or our waitress—to bother talking about ourselves. It was always an escape. We would challenge each other to do the stupidest things. Try to drink soup with a fork. Use our opposite hand to eat. Write a thirty-second commercial segment advertising the restaurant. Fit as much food into our mouths as we could and try to say a comprehensible sentence. We embraced eternal immaturity.

I shake my head at the memory. What was wrong with that relationship? Or, worse, was everything right? Maybe Dylan's always going to come in first. Everybody else will have to settle for a distant second.

I stare across the table at Kari and I'm completely turned off. She's gorgeous and sweet, but I feel nervous around her, and by the time the steak comes I barely have an appetite.

Kari starts talking about family and then she hits me with:

"So, Gray, do you want to have kids?" I sit up straighter. This is worse than small talk. This is serious relationship talk and we're not even through our official screening date yet.

"Uh," I say. I smooth the napkin on my lap and stall. I want to tell her I'm only nineteen years old and parenthood isn't an impending concern of mine at the moment.

"I want five kids," she announces, and stares me up and down like she's evaluating my sperm strength. "Three boys and two girls. I already have their names picked out," she says.

I tell her that's great. I tell her I love kids, which I do, not that I want to procreate any time soon. Then, she informs me she wants to live in the Southwest to stay close to her parents. She thinks Yuma, Arizona has a lot of potential and would be a great community for raising a family. She likes small towns. She eyes me critically over the rim of her glass. She wants to know what I think about this.

I think you're scaring the hell out of me.

"I prefer big cities," I say.

"I would consider a big city," she says, "if there was a decent income coming in." She raises a thin eyebrow. "Do you plan on playing professional baseball after college?" she asks, pretending it's a casual question, but I know what she's getting at. I play my get-out-of-jail-free card.

"No," I say.

She frowns. "What do you want to do?"

"Actually, I think I want to be a gym teacher," I say. Her eyes fall, so do her shoulders, and even her chest loses some of its giddy sparkle.

I have to contain my smile. I'm off the hook. She's no longer interested and for the first time tonight, I'm beginning to enjoy myself. Hopefully she won't want dessert. Too fattening.

***

I drop Kari off an hour later. I'm tired from forcing too much conversation, crabby from a date that bombed and sixty-forty dollars poorer with nothing to show for it. And my steak was overcooked. Not that I'm feeling sorry for myself.

I end up driving down Sage Street, like a magnetic force pulled my car in this direction. I slow down when I pass Dylan's apartment and see a light through the curtains. It's soft and welcoming and before I know it, I park along the curb. I hear music coming from inside as I walk up the cobblestone pathway to her door. I knock and she yells to come in.

Dylan is sitting cross-legged on the floor with a mess of photos spread out around her. She's wearing a pink tank top, gray sweatpants and bright blue, fuzzy socks that look like fur. I already feel my mood lightening, just walking into her world.

"What's up?" she ask as she turns down the stereo.

I point at her socks. "How many Muppets did they have to kill to make those?" I wonder.

She gives me one of her killer smiles and it makes me shrink back. Why can't Kari have this effect on me? It would be so much more convenient. But if love were convenient there wouldn't be millions of songs and movies and books obsessing over it, or therapists and doctors consoling all the people falling in and out of it.

I walk around the edge of the room, taking in the simple, open space, and tell her I was in the neighborhood. She scoots over and makes room for me on the rug. I stare at the space next to her. What happened to my brilliant avoidance plan? That idea lasted a whole twenty-four hours. Amazing self-discipline, Gray.

I slump down on the floor and lean against the edge of the futon. I notice her critiquing my outfit.

"Fancy date?" she asks. I ignore her question and pick up one of the pictures hogging the floor space. It's just a shot of a tree trunk.

"What are all these for?" I ask, and she tells me she's making a scrapbook for her grandma's birthday.

"Cat helped me get a few baby-sitting jobs so I could afford to print them out."

I examine the black and white photograph. At first I'm not very impressed, but as I look closer, it appears Dylan climbed the tree and took the shot from inside the branches, angled up to the sky to catch the overhanging leaves. All the knots of the bark are exposed and textured by sunlight, and it looks like old, leathery skin, wrinkled with age. It gives it this human quality. Something about the picture is tranquil. Fantastical. I want to walk inside the shot and lie underneath all the contrasts of light and dark.

"It's taken from a squirrel's point of view," she says. I ask her what she means and she tells me it was a creative challenge she gave herself. For a day she tried to capture images from a squirrel's perspective. She climbed trees. She took pictures from the ground. She ran out in front of moving cars. The more I look at her photos the more I see what she means. She hands me one and explains how she crawled underneath a dog's head to take a picture of the bottom of its mouth. Its droopy jowls take up most of the shot and a shiny, quizzical eye peers down at the camera lens.

I look at her and smile. She flinches a little, like I jolted her with an electric shock.

"What's wrong?" I ask. She's just staring at me, all wide-eyed and surprised.

"That's the first time you've smiled at me since I've been back," she says.

I wrinkle my eyebrows at this. "That's not true."

"Believe me, I would know. I thought I'd get at least a grin from the crack I made about bull testicles."

I smile again and she stares at my mouth like she's never seen my face look happy before.

"Wow," she says. She touches my face. The motion is so fast it takes me by surprise and before I can lean away, she lightly runs her fingers over my cheek, to the edge of my lips. Something catches in my chest. I stare back at her and my entire body heats up. I feel the heat of her fingers travel through my skin, between my bones, tugging on the tissue around my heart.

"Sorry," she says and drops her hand. "I just missed that." We both sit there, quiet, the air in the room electrified. Something inside of me is shifting again and this time I can't fight it.

Not good. I suck in a deep breath. She looks away and clears her throat. It sounds as tight as mine feels.

She picks up a few more photos and starts to explain them to me. I try to focus on what she's saying, not on this feeling in my stomach, this suffocating feeling like if I don't touch her I'll die.

She hands a picture to me that she says was staged. It's taken from a gravel road with a car heading straight for her. Her camera is aimed up at the fender and tires and there are two guys in the front seat. They have these surprised looks on their faces, like they're about to hit her. It's perfect.

"These are really great, Dylan."

"It was a fun way to spend a day," she says. I try and imagine her wasting a single day. I don't think she could.

"Have you ever tried selling these?"

"I'd feel bad charging my grandma."

I roll my eyes. "No, I mean in a gallery."

Dylan looks down at her pictures. "It's just a hobby. Anyone can do this," she says.

I shake my head. "Some people go to school for years to try to learn to be half as creative as you naturally are. I'm just saying, if you're good at something, figure out a way to make money doing it."

"That sounds mean."

I smile at her. "It's not mean to take money from people, Dylan. It's called a job."

"You can't make a living at everything," she says, but it sounds more like a challenge.

"Sure you can."

She taps her chin with one finger. "Okay, let's say I love riding bikes. How do I get paid to ride bikes?"

I start counting off reasons on my fingers. "You work at a bike shop, and you eventually open up your own store. You ride professionally. You lead sight-seeing bike tours. There are lots of ways."

Dylan sets her hand on my arm. "Let's say I love walking and eating ice cream at the same time—"

I grab her hand in mine. "No, I'm not going on one of your random thought crusades. I just wanted to point out your pictures are really amazing. I'd love to see the world from your eyes for a day."

I let go of her fingers, but I can't shift my eyes away from hers even though I want to, even though I can hear a siren going off in my mind. This is exactly why I avoided being alone with her. Right next to her. The energy is too strong.

"I mostly picture everybody naked," she says.

"Really? I'm jealous," I say. She smiles and I smile and my heart is jamming away in my chest.

"I'm jealous of your world sometimes," she admits. "Of all these people that get to be in your life everyday. Make you laugh. Date you. It makes me realize how much of you I'm missing out on."

"My life is rooted down," I remind her. "You'd hate that."

She leans forward to collect her pictures in a pile. I ask the question that's been gnawing at me since Dylan showed up, passed out at my front door. The question that made me pull the car over and walk into temptation. Because I need to know.

"Dylan, of all the places to go after Europe, why did you come to Albuquerque?"

She rests her head against the futon and stares at the wall in front of us. I drink in her profile. Her arm's touching mine. I feel like I'm sitting too close to a fire. Like it might scorch my skin.

"You're here," she says. "You're my hang glider."

"I'm, what?"

She takes a long breath and exhales slowly. Dylan hardly ever talks about herself. But she knows I deserve an explanation. "I was trying to figure out what felt like home to me. It should have been Wisconsin or my family. At least my dogs. But all I could think about was you."

She turns to look at me and there's a confused look on her face, like even she doesn't understand it.

"You wanted to see me more than your own family?"

"I love my parents, but they give me such a hard time."

"They're your family," I say. "They're supposed to give you a hard time."

"I guess," Dylan says. She picks at a piece of loose thread on the rug. She tells me it's more than that. It's like they're trying to change her. "Every time I go home, my mom tells me I need to figure out my life, which to her just means settling down and domesticating."

"Domesticating?" I ask.

"Yeah, you know. Married, part-time cook, part-time housekeeper, mother of 2.3 kids."

"Got it," I say.

"My sister thinks I'm fashion-challenged. She wants me to cut my hair and buy new clothes and wear jeans that are tight which just give me wedgies. I like loose fitting jeans because they're easy to bend down and take pictures in."

"In case you feel like being a squirrel for a day," I point out. Her eyes light up.

"Exactly. But they don't get it. They don't see *me*. They just see this silly daydreamer with no ambition, like I'm lost in the world trying to find myself. They don't get that this is who I am. Just because I'm not anchored down doesn't mean I'm lost. I really wish people could understand that."

I look down at her photos and think about this. "They're probably worried when you're gone all the time," I say. "They care about you."

"I just get tired of having to explain myself every time I turn around. Especially to my own family. I feel like they should support me." Her face falls into an adorable pout. "And all my dad wants to talk about is college and savings accounts and whether or not I have health insurance."

I smile widely at the frown on her face. "You mean they want you to think about real life?"

"That's their idea of life. It isn't mine," she says. "My dad never asks me about the places I go. He doesn't ask to see my pictures. That's real life to me. That's what I'm proud of."

I rest my elbow on my knee and think about this. I tell Dylan it's strange because parents wait their whole lives for us to finally grow up and be independent. Then, as soon as we become adults, they panic and try to reel us back in. They don't know how to let us make our own decisions because they don't want to see us fail. They want to protect us. But they have to let us make mistakes. I suddenly feel bad for parents. It can't be an easy job.

"So," Dylan continues, "When I decided to come home, I wanted to be with you. Because you've never once tried to change me or force me to settle down or ask me why I take pictures all day or why I can't focus on one thought for more than five seconds. I'm learning that's pretty rare."

She rests her boney knee against mine and I'm frozen by how that tiny amount of contact feels like electricity.

"Remember how easy last summer was?" she asks. I keep my eyes safely away from hers and nod. "It was just you and me, everyday," she says. "No obligations, no responsibilities."

"Hey, Video Hutch was extremely important to me," I argue.

She stares up at the ceiling and smiles. I glance at her profile, a face I've studied longer than any book, any lesson. And just like that, I'm in love with her again. I let my guard down for two seconds and this is what happens. I wonder if she can sense it and if Dylan's anything like I remember, she can.

"I wish we could go back there. Just you and me and the desert," she says.

"Our house on Camelback," I say.

She nods. "Boba."

I lift my hand and trace a finger down Dylan's arm.

I swallow. It's so easy. Her lips are inches away from mine. I can smell her skin. I close my eyes. I think about song lyrics. *It Ain't Me Babe*, by Bob Dylan. *Don't Come Around Here No More*, by Tom Petty. I let the words try to talk sense into me.

"I should go," I say. It's barely been a week. I need to be stronger than this. I need to be the one calling the shots. I can't just give into the moment.

I stand up and Dylan's watching me. Her face is flushed and there's a question in her eyes I can read.

"I've been thinking about all this," I say. "About us." She waits for me to continue. I tuck my hands in my front pockets and stare at my feet. "Maybe we can try to just be friends."

I glance down at her and there's this surprised look in her eyes. "Friends?" She thinks about this for a few seconds. "We could try that," she says, but her face is doubtful.

"I've never tried to be friends with any of my exes," I add.

"Exes." She says the word out loud with a blank look on her face.

"Yeah, but maybe it could work."

She narrows her eyes for a moment, like she's testing me. "Sure. Friends." She stands up, reaches her hand out and we shake on it. Just shaking her hand makes me want to pull her against me.

"As long as you still let me love you," she says.

I let go of her hand. "You love everyone, Dylan."

I downplay her words. I dilute the meaning because it's my only way to beat her.

"Okay," she says. "Just so you know." She says goodnight and I shut the door behind me.

Dylan

I stare at the door and try to mentally digest what just happened. Friends? He seriously expects me to be his friend? I don't want to have sex with my friends. I don't look at my friends and think they are God's sexiest creation. I don't want to rip the clothes off of my friends and marry my friends. I don't want to grow old with my friends until we're withered like raisins.

Does Gray think love comes with a dial you can use to control how strong the current flows? Is he trying to keep it on low when I want to crank it to extreme? Who wants to live on a low voltage? Where's the fun in that?

I sigh and fall back on the futon. I want to stand outside Gray's window and blare the chorus of *Strange Currencies* so REM can explain how I feel using lyrics and melodramatic guitar chords. I want more than his forgiveness. I want more than his trust. I want all of him.

"Can we at least be friends with benefits?" I say to the ceiling.

Gray

Friends. Brilliant fucking cop-out, Gray. Like you can keep your hands off of her. If life came with an audience, mine would be laughing hysterically right now.

I drive down the road and consider my offer. It was a desperate idea that seemed right at the time. But more than anything, I just panicked. Note to self: *Do not make relationship decisions under the influence of sexual frustration.*

Friends. Is that even remotely possible?

Can you control how much you love someone? Maybe I can try. It's a psychological research experiment and I've volunteered myself as the lucky guinea pig. Yay, me.

I mentally list reasons why I can be friends with Dylan. Reason one: I'm not really attracted to her anymore. Okay, who am I kidding? I want to touch her every second I'm next to her. And when I'm not next to her. Scratch that one.

Reason two: I'll hardly see her, between school and games and studying.

Reason three: I'll date other women (hopefully with more success).

Reason four: Dylan doesn't have a cell phone, so it's not like I can get in touch with her that easily.

I turn up the volume of my stereo and tap my fingers on the steering wheel.

Friends. It *could* happen.

I nod to myself and feel safe with this new plan. As long as I'm calling the shots, I can handle this. I just need the upper hand. I make the plays. I set the dates. I draw the boundaries. That's how I keep her at arm's length. And my heart safe.

Gray

It's our third Sunday night dinner and the word has gotten out. Our guest list has grown, so Dylan sets up a folding table next to the kitchen table. A few more guys from the team show up. Travis continues to invite himself over, and Dylan brings Cat with her this time, which gets Miles so worked up he barely eats. Todd invites his girlfriend, Liz. They've been dating since high school. Liz always looks perfect, like she gets out of bed in the morning with her blond hair parted and her bangs neatly aligned. Her outfits make her look like a walking Old Navy commercial. She's getting her teaching certificate, and she's always busying volunteering at their church and leading bible studies and organizing food drives. Her name should be Linda.

We're all sitting around the table digesting and suddenly Todd clears his throat and says he has news.

"Liz and I are engaged," he blurts.

Everyone's silent and I look around to see Bubba shocked, Miles amused, and Dylan impressed. I stare back at Todd like he's nuts. They're only twenty years old! They can't get married. Then again, I proposed to Dylan last summer. But that wasn't real. I don't think. Maybe? No.

Dylan's voice cuts through the stifled silence and she makes a toast. Everyone's taking turns congratulating them. Todd says they're having a judge perform the ceremony. It's going to be simple, with only their parents, because they can't afford a big wedding. They're going to throw a dinner party at Liz's parents' house to celebrate and we're all invited. It's the Sunday over Memorial Day weekend, one of the few days we have off from our game schedule.

Wow. I'm officially old. Have we really hit the marriage zone?

Dylan's keeping the conversation going and asks all the right questions and Liz is beaming and Todd is all proud. For some reason, I'm annoyed. Bored. But also jealous. I look across the table at these two friends who have found it: life-long love. I wonder why some people get to experience it, and some don't and some trip over it and break apart and die with broken hearts. I wonder who chooses our destiny, if it's a god, or fate, or karmic luck. I look at Dylan across the table. She looks beautiful as she smiles for them and celebrates with them and I wonder why I'm not enough for her unconditional love.

After dinner we start cleaning up. Miles is flirting with Cat, Bubba's doing dishes with Lenny, and Todd and Liz are sitting side-by-side on the couch watching reality TV, like the boring married couple they're soon to become. All these people look so happy and satisfied that it's making me sick.

I can barely look at Dylan because it makes something hollow unfurl. And it aches.

Dylan

"Come on Dylan, just get it over with," Gray tells me.

I persuaded Gray to come with me today, to be my wing man as I show my photography, for the first time, to a local gallery. Gray told me he knows a little bit about the business since his sister worked in a gallery for two years, so he penciled me into his schedule for a quick hour. It's a rare window of time he's giving me these days. He seems to be going out of his way to avoid me.

He's walking down the block towards the gallery, but I'm stalling. I remind Gray I've never done anything like this before. He tells me he has my back.

"Just be your confident self," he says. "Hold your head up high and make them think they should be thanking you for even considering them. It's all in the attitude."

Normally I am confident, but it's different with my photography. It's like handing over a piece of my soul to be criticized. I look through the glass windows at elegant black and white photos on the walls outlined in sleek, black frames, showcased under bright spotlights.

"Maybe I should start smaller," I say. "I could put up some prints in a coffee shop, or a restaurant or a Laundromat."

Gray stops at the door and looks at me. "A Laundromat?"

I shrug. "Maybe it's an untapped market."

"If people can't afford a washer and dryer, I doubt they invest in much original artwork," he informs me as he opens the glass door.

I tuck my portfolio under my arm and take a deep breath. We walk into a room that smells upscale, like polish and perfume and the lighting is amazing and I'm way out of league.

"Can I help you?" a woman behind the counter says to us. She's older, with curly gray hair and long silver earrings that sway back and forth. She regards me carefully, her eyes scanning my clothes and my face. I walk up to the counter and set my portfolio down between us, next to a glass vase full of colorful wild flowers. A few quiet seconds crawl by.

"That's a beautiful flower arrangement," I finally say and point to the vase and the woman thanks me. I start to turn around because I can't go through with this, but Gray blocks me with his leg and keeps my feet pinned between him and the counter. I take a deep breath.

"My name's Dylan and I'm interested in showcasing some of my photography here," I say quickly so I can get it all out.

She smiles at me, but it's a sympathetic smile that makes me cringe.

"We aren't looking for new clients at the moment," she says. "There's a waiting list for wall space so we have to be very selective." She doesn't even glance at my album. "We also only take photographers with professional experience," she says. "The owner makes the final decision, but I screen the photos first."

My mouth is drying up. Is it just me, or is there not enough oxygen in this room? And why is it suddenly a hundred degrees? I nod and turn to leave again, but Gray grabs my arm tight and holds me in place.

"Why don't you at least take a look?" Gray asks and slides the portfolio closer to her. "Before you pass up an opportunity?" He squeezes my arm with encouragement before he lets it go. I figure, at the very least, Gray is touching me again. It's not a complete waste of an afternoon.

She glances down at the binder and back at me. She asks me where I went to school for photography.

"Uh," I stammer. "Mesa Community College," I say. She waits for me to continue so I lie and tell her I also had an apprenticeship with a nature photographer in California, but he's pretty exclusive so she's probably never heard of him. In my defense, this is partly true. I spent a few days traveling around with my friend Jake, in Shasta County. He just didn't happen to be a professional and I was the one training him.

"How old are you?" she asks. I bluff.

"Twenty-three." I widen my shoulders as if this will make me look older.

She makes a ticking sound with her tongue that is god-awful intimidating. "That's pretty young," she says. "Most of our photographers are veterans in the business. All of them have some sort of background, either print work or online."

"She also works with me," Gray adds, "for a magazine." He gives her his most charming smile. I notice her features soften a little; it's a calming effect Gray's smile generally has on women. I step in while we have a window of a chance.

"Right," I say. "We work for—"

"An independent weekly," he says. "Published in—"

"Wisconsin," I finish.

Gray tightens his lips together and glances at me.

"Interesting," she says. "What brings you two all the way to New Mexico?"

Gray starts. "We're…doing a spread on—"

"Pueblo community life in the Southwest," I finish.

Gray and I both shut our traps before we have to spread another lie, but this woman looks amused. She picks up my portfolio and starts to flip through the pictures. I describe the theme, that it's a series of shots taken from a squirrel's perspective and her face is deadpan. She looks up at me and I wait for her to call me a liar and throw me out of her store. Maybe first she'll clonk me on the head with my album.

She opens her mouth to comment and every muscle in my neck tenses up.

"How much do you charge for your prints?" she asks. I stare back at her and my mouth falls open. Gray pokes me in the back.

"It varies," I say. I have no clue.

"We don't have space for these in the gallery right now, but I know someone who would love them. She's obsessed with squirrels. I think she feeds half of this city's population." I expect her to give me a phone number, but instead she just yells.

"Mary, get out here and see this!"

Gray and I exchange glances.

Another woman walks out, older, probably in her late sixties, a veil of sophistication suspended in the air around her. She's wearing a fitted black blazer and slacks. Her thin hair is dyed light blond and there's so much hair-spray not a single strand moves when she walks. My eyes fall to her feet, which are dressed in red moccasins. Her shoes make me smile. I might have a chance.

She grabs my portfolio and I explain my theme again. She stares me up and down and sifts through the photos in record speed. I watch the diamond rings on her fingers sparkle in the light as she flips her wrist. Then, something catches her eye and she slows down. She goes back over each photo, one by one and minutes go by without a word. I'm sweating.

"Very creative," she says and she reaches out her hand and introduces herself as Mary, the owner of the gallery. Then she introduces the woman behind the counter, Barb, as her assistant.

She holds the album against her chest and taps her red fingernails on the leather. "These would go great in my office," she says and Barb nods. Mary gives me a critical stare. "How much for the set?" she asks.

I bite my bottom lip and look at Gray for help.

Gray leans his hand casually on the counter and creases his forehead. "What was your last offer?" he asks me. "I forget."

A competitive fire sparks Mary's light blue eyes. I finally see what sets this woman off. I'm wondering if fifty dollars is too much to ask.

"I'll give you a hundred and fifty for the set," she offers.

"A hundred and fifty dollars?" I say, shocked.

Barb interjects. "Mary, don't take advantage of the poor girl. That's great work. I've never seen anything like it."

"Fine," Mary says. "One seventy-five."

I'm in over my head and then Gray opens his mouth. "Didn't someone offer you two hundred?" he asks me.

I stare back at Mary and try to look modest.

She narrows her eyes but I see determination behind them. "How many photos are in here?"

"Eighteen," I say.

"Fine, two-fifty."

Two hundred and fifty dollars!? I don't know where I get the nerve to do this, but I raise the stakes.

"With one more agreement," I say.

"What's that?"

"Let me show some of my photos here. I'd like some wall space, please," I say.

Mary and Barb exchange glances and Barbs asks if I do portraits.

I shake my head. "I'm not a fan of posed pictures," I say. "I like catching people when they're being natural. When they don't expect it. Portraits are too forced. It isn't authentic to me."

"So what do you prefer to do?" Mary asks and she seems intrigued.

"Anything. People. Animals. Landscapes. Architecture." I tell them about one of my favorite series I did recently. It's a set where I've taken pictures of people either caught in genuine laughter, or frozen in pouts. I tell them it's a mix of all ages. I explain my favorite picture, taken of a boy I caught sitting in the back of a truck and—

"Give her some space," Mary decides.

Barb glances through her desk calendar. "In six weeks I can fit you in."

"Give her fifteen spaces for the set she just described. There's wall space in the back showroom. We'll squeeze her in now."

"Fine," Barb says. "I can fit you in for our show next Friday," she says. "Come three days in advance with fifteen of your best shots, all eight by eleven. Keep it to all color or all black and white. We take thirty-five percent of the sales." She hands me a sheet with the terms, pricing and selling conditions and tells me to read it over and sign it when I come back.

"That's it?" I say.

Gray senses my question and steps in. "Can you explain how your shows run? Every gallery's a little different." Mary explains they have two Friday night showings a month with drinks and appetizers.

"Come the opening night of your show and be ready to market yourself," she tells me. "Work the room. It's a big deal when the artist takes the time to show up. People love having a face to go with the art they buy. It gives them more to talk about when they show it off."

"And you're gorgeous," Barb says. I feel my face redden at the compliment. "So get your face in the crowd. I think you're the youngest photographer we've ever had."

"But I'd wear something more presentable," Mary offers as she looks at my jeans and dirty flip flops. "A skirt will be fine. And some heels."

Gray nods. "Definitely a skirt," he says.

I try not to wince. I have to go clothes shopping?

"I assume you'll accept cash for these?" Mary asks. She taps the portfolio in her hand.

"Cash works just fine," I tell her.

She coordinates a time for me to drop off the pictures and Gray is writing down all the details because I've lost all cognitive skills. My mind is floating in a dream-fog.

We step out of the Desert Sky Gallery and I'm two-hundred and fifty dollars richer, but that doesn't even compare with the fact that someone loves my pictures. And sees potential. And I have a show. My first gallery show.

I grab Gray's hand and pull him down the street, half skipping, and tell him we need to celebrate.

"I have an idea," I say. "Let's have a Peep-eating contest. My treat." I start rambling about how the bunny Peeps are better than the chicken Peeps, and how they've come out with chocolate mousse flavored Peeps that look disgusting but maybe we should give them a try. I wait for Gray to respond, but he's looking at my hand wrapped around his and his eyebrows are raised. I hate that he's so annoyed by my touch. I drop his hand with a frown.

"Sorry," I say. "Habit."

"It's alright." He walks a little ahead of me. I sigh as I watch the unnatural distance between us grow. This is ridiculous. Did we time warp back to eighth grade?

"Oh, ow!" I yell and cover my mouth with my hand. Gray's turning to unlock his car door but he stops and looks at me.

"What?"

"Ow," I moan and I keep my hand tight on my mouth. "I just bit my lip." I stop walking and Gray studies me.

"You're fine," he says.

"It really hurts. I taste blood."

He walks up to me and tries to move my hand but I keep it rigid against my mouth.

"No," I mutter through my fingers. He leans his head down to get a closer look and fights to pull my hand away, his eyes genuinely concerned. I wait until he's an inch closer, then I drop my hand, arch my feet and press my lips against his. Before he can react, I wrap my arms around his neck to pull his head down closer to mine and try to hold my lips against his as long as it will last. It's rough and forced and it's not going to win an award for the most glamorous kiss of all times, but it's a start. Gray yanks my hands off his neck and his blue eyes are inches from mine, shooting bullets.

"You lying, manipulating little—"

But he cuts himself off and slams his lips hard against mine and I can barely keep my legs steady because something powerful is rushing through my system. He drags me into the alley and we stumble and I can hear a radiator buzzing next to us. He pushes me against the brick wall. I pull him closer until his chest is pressed against mine. His baseball cap flops off his head and lands somewhere by our feet.

I squeeze my eyes shut and I want to cry because this kiss doesn't come close to my memory. It's a million times better.

***

By the time we make it back to his car, our faces are flushed and my legs are shaky. I steal glances at Gray while he drives me home. His lips are raw and red from making out for an hour.

Only one thought fills my mind. That was amazing.

I reach my hand out to touch his lips but Gray leans away from my fingers.

"That was a mistake," he says.

His words snap me out of my trance and I stare at his defiant expression. True, I attacked him, but he definitely didn't fight me. There were two people kissing back there, for an hour. And he has the nerve to call the greatest moment of the year a mistake? He pulls up to my driveway and I wait for him to look at me, but his eyes are focused out the window. Coward.

"Should we talk about this?" I ask.

Gray mumbles that he needs to get to practice. I stare out at my apartment. I don't push it and I don't argue because I know what he needs when his heart is warring with his mind. Time.

I get out of the car and watch him peel out of the driveway. I hear rap music loudly curse the air. I can't help but smile as his car disappears down the street. I noticed his hands adjust his shorts in the car, to hide something slightly obvious in his pants. Okay, so he's still attracted to me. Check that one off my list. Now, time to bring down those walls.

Gray

"If you want any control over this, then whatever you do, do not have sex with her," Bubba warns me.

We're all sitting around the living room watching *Transformers,* which invariably leads to discussing having sex with Megan Fox, which broadens to sex talk in general. I stare at him. Bubba, of all people, is telling me to avoid sex? These are the most contradictory words he has ever spoken.

"Don't even think about having sex," Bubba says. "It's a dead end. She'll get you right where she wants you and then she'll start calling all the shots. Sex gives women complete control."

Miles throws a ratty couch pillow, hitting Bubba on the side of the head.

"Are you hearing yourself?" Miles says. "You have no business dishing out advice you could never take."

"Women have three ultimate powers we will always succumb to," Bubba insists. "Two boobs and one vagina."

"What?" I say.

"It's true. Their bodies are their number one weapon. They know we can't get enough of them. No matter how big or small or round or skinny they are. We don't care. We're so simple minded, Gray. They think we're so hard to figure out. Well, we're not. We're pathetically predictable.

We just want unlimited access to their bodies, and we'll do anything to get it. We'll buy flowers and write poems and take dance classes and pretend we enjoy window shopping and act like we notice their haircuts, but in the end, we do it for the nookie. It's how we're wired."

"You're nuts," Todd says. Bubba ignores him and continues with his theory.

"Then, when they've got us latched into their choke collars, they turn it all around and call sex love and love sex and they screw with our minds so we don't know the difference. It's all a cruel conspiracy, man."

I laugh out loud at this.

"That's really romantic," Todd says. "It's a wonder why you can't maintain a healthy relationship."

"Hey, virgin boy, we're talking about sex right now. Something you know nothing about, so you have no opinion on the matter."

"I think you two should get back together," Miles says. "Dylan's great. And she's hot."

"You think all women are hot," I say.

"Dude, Dylan is a fox. Are you blind?" Bubba interjects. I raise my eyebrows at this. Are we talking about the same Dylan? My tall, gangly, hyper—

"The hippie look is hot," Bubba says.

"She could be a model," Miles says. I turn to see Todd nodding.

"And she has no idea how good looking she is, which is extra hot," Todd agrees.

I look down at the floor, shocked. They're actually talking about Dylan. *My* Dylan. She's always been too busy trying to embarrass me in social situations for me to see this apparently unanimous fact.

"Gray, I'm telling you, if you have sex, all it will do is remind you what you're giving up. Sex always wins. It's a survival mechanism for all relationships. Why do you think people get married?"

"Because they're in love?" I reason.

"No," Bubba says. "It's so they can get laid on a regular basis. Why do you think Todd's rushing into his wedding with Liz? So he can pick out lampshades with someone?"

Todd rolls his eyes, but I also notice he doesn't argue.

"Gray, if you don't want anything to happen with Dylan, just say no. Pass on the ass. No love, not even with the glove. Block the cock."

"Okay, I get it," I laugh. "No getting physical."

My phone beeps and I open it to find a message from Kari. She asks me if I want to hang out this weekend. I groan and wonder out loud why she's still pursuing this.

Bubba frowns at me. "You're dumping a girl after one bad date?" I nod and he shakes his head. "Dude, if you're determined to get over Dylan, you've got to date," he says. "Besides, first dates don't count. They're always lame, it's like an interview."

I stare down at my phone and think about this. "So what's the second date going to be like?" I ask.

"Like a follow-up interview," he says.

"Sounds great," I say. The memory of our first date still makes me shudder.

"My first three dates with Amy were painful," Bubba admits. "But we ended up dating for over a year."

"What changed after the third date?" I ask.

"We had sex," he said simply. I shake my head and think maybe I should reconsider taking any of Bubba's relationship advice.

Dylan

"This is so stupid," I say. "Can't he see we're destined to be together?"

Cat, Lenny and I are hanging out in Cat's backyard. I've been trying to take pictures to get my mind off of Gray, but nothing helps. It's been three days and I haven't heard from him, seen him. Kissed him.

"Sounds like a bad case of sexual tension," Cat offers. "Maybe you just need to get to the meat of this. Pun intended."

I stop pacing and stare at her. "I need him to mildly like me first."

"What exactly do you want out of this, Dylan?" Lenny asks. She watches me with a cigarette poised between her fingers.

I slump down on the grass. "I want him to give me a second chance. He hasn't told me to leave, so I know he still feels something. It's not over between us."

"Here's the thing," Cat says. "You two have already been intimate. So, if he's really over you then the sex won't compare to what it used to be. Either you'll realize your feelings have faded and you'll both be able to move on. Or," she continues, "The more likely scenario, you'll realize all the passion is still there and you'll stop wasting time and get back together. It's a win-win situation."

I curl my fingers around thick blades of grass until I rip out a clump in each of my hands. "I can't have sex with him if it doesn't love me," I say. "Is there an option B?"

"You could hook up with someone else. My mom always told me the best way to get over a guy is to get on top of another one," Lenny says.

"Your *mother* gave you that advice?" Cat asks.

"Best advice she ever gave me."

"Lovely," I say.

"Make out with Travis," Lenny says. "He thinks you're hot."

I roll over on my side and glare at Lenny. "I am not touching Travis. He's a tool. He probably has a mirror over his bed."

I sigh and stare up at the sky. I comment that one of the clouds looks like a bowl full of popcorn. They both ignore my observation.

"What if you try to make Gray jealous?" Cat asks. "That might speed things up." I glance at her doubtfully and ask how I'm supposed to do that.

"Wait," Lenny says and sits up straighter. "I know. Travis comes into the Brew House every day at the same time. If you just happen to be there and Gray just happens to walk in and see you two together..."

Cat slams her hand on the grass. "Brilliant," she says. Before I can open my mouth up to argue, they're already discussing what I'm going to wear for my date of betrayal.

Gray

Five days later I still can't get Dylan out of my head. She planted a seed and it's growing and invading my thoughts.

But where is this going to go? I tried to stay away from her and that didn't work. I tried to be just friends. Fail. What if we become friends with benefits? Just two quirky kids that meet up for a fling every summer? Can I make Dylan that easily interchangeable?

I walk into the Brew House because I have to unload on someone, and I know Lenny will be only too happy to hear me admit I'm still in love with Dylan. When I walk in, Lenny has this weird look on her face, something close to guilt. I walk up to the counter and ask her what's wrong.

"You didn't get my text?" she asks.

I shake my head and tell her my phone's turned off. She says she sent me a code red, which means I need to drop everything I'm doing and call her. She's only used a code red on me twice—one night when she got a flat tire, and one morning when she had to perform a major walk of shame and needed emotional support (and an extra pair of shoes since she managed to lose hers).

My mouth drops open and I think the worst. "Did you get fired?"

She rolls her eyes. "I wish."

"Did you poison a football player?" (a threat she continually promises to follow through with).

"Shh. No." She shifts her eyes and I follow her stare to the back of the room. First I grin because I see Dylan, but then I blink and I swear she's sitting at a table with Travis, but I must be seeing things. I blink again, but he's still there so I blink one more time and then my eyes widen because I see his hand touch her fucking leg. My primitive caveman instinct slams into territorial mode. It's war time.

I glare at Lenny like this is all her fault.

"Don't look at me," she says. "I don't condone this kind of behavior. They didn't show up together, if it makes you feel any better. But they've been sitting there for two hours so I thought it was time to combine forces."

I ball my hands into a fist and my blood is racing. I swear steam is rising from my body. Travis Toolshed Taylor? Is she *serious*?

"Gray, take a few deep breaths. You have a little bit of an angry streak."

I ignore her as I walk towards the happy stupid couple. All these thoughts are racing through my head. Does Travis actually like Dylan? Or is he just using her to piss me off? Could Dylan be even remotely attracted to a self-absorbed prick like Travis? He could be the poster boy for Oscar Mayer, he's such a meathead. And what does he see in Dylan? She's not his type. He goes for tall, skinny, sexy… shit. She is completely his type.

When I approach the table Dylan looks away from the laptop she and Toolshed were peering into. She smiles at me and it's this innocent smile like she was hoping to run into me so I could be the third wheel on their little coffee date.

"Hey!" she says. Travis turns around and he smiles too. As I stare back and forth between them, their future passes before my eyes like a montage sequence: A wedding invitation announcing Travis and Dylan's wedding. A birth announcement arrives, introducing me to their healthy baby boy, Travis Jr. I see their dream house: a two story brick home with a red minivan in the driveway, a white picket fence and a mailbox with birds painted on it to receive all the happy mail for the Travis and Dylan happy abode.

"Gray?" Dylan asks and there's worry in her voice. "You okay?"

I blink back at her and she tells me Travis is helping her build a website for her photography.

"It's not as hard as I thought," she says and Travis leans in and smiles coolly.

"You just have a good teacher," he says. She turns to me and asks if I want to sit down.

I can practically hear my blood rushing to my head. "Can I talk to you for a second?" I ask, fighting to keep my voice steady.

"Sure." She shifts her chair around until she faces me. She's wearing a shirt that actually fits. It hugs her chest and brings out the green in her eyes. I don't want Travis to have that kind of luxury view.

"Outside," I say.

Dylan follows me out the door. I walk down the block because I need a few seconds to cool off. It doesn't help. I still want to scream. I turn and glare at her when she catches up to me.

"Travis Toolshed Taylor? Are you kidding me?"

She raises her eyebrows. "That's not really his middle name, is it?"

I throw my hands up with exasperation. "Of all the guys in this state, you're on a date with the one guy who's so stupid—"

She puts a hand on her hip. "First of all, it's not a date. I was sitting there, minding my own business, well, actually eavesdropping on these two girls at the table next to me who were discussing this new salt-free diet they're trying—"

"Focus, Dylan," I say. I press my fingers against my temples and close my eyes because I feel a brain aneurysm coming on.

"Sorry. Anyway, he showed up and invited himself to sit down."

"And then he just happened to rub your leg," I point out.

"What?"

"Why are you dressed like that?" I ask. Dylan stares down at her jeans, which I'm displeased to see also fit. She's never worn jeans like that around me. They actually show off her body. She looks up at me like I'm insane.

She explains Liz donated a bag of clothes to the dress-Dylan-fund. She tells me they're all really nice and they actually fit. I have to interrupt her again because she's diverting the conversation.

"I don't want you hanging around Travis," I say. "He's an asshole."

"He's your teammate. You shouldn't talk about him like that."

"If I ever see you alone with him again—"

"Wait just one minute, Gray Thomas," she holds her hand up to cut me off. "If I recall correctly, it was you who passed me off as single right in front of Travis, so this isn't exactly my fault. *Or* his. It's none of your business what I do with Travis Tooltime Taylor."

I glare at her and take a deep breath. "Toolshed," I correct her. "Not Tooltime."

"Second of all," she continues, "you've made it perfectly clear you don't want our relationship to go anywhere. You don't love me anymore. You're over me. And that's fine because I'll settle for being your friend, if that's what it takes to have you in my life. But if you get to be single, then guess what, so do I."

I bite my lips at this realization. I hate the idea of Dylan with other guys. It's worse than anything. "Then what happened last week?"

She points a finger at me. "*You* told *me* it didn't mean anything."

My heart's beating so hard I can feel it pulse in my neck. It meant everything.

"I guess I was right," I say. I turn and walk away and I hear Dylan call after me, but I ignore her. I turn down the block and take out my phone. Two can play the jealousy game.

Revenge is on. So what if Dylan had one lousy date? Girls throw their phone numbers at me on a daily basis, like I'm a lottery ticket for someone to win. I scroll down my phone list until I find Kari's name. I send her a message asking if she wants to hang out tomorrow.

She responds in under ten seconds.

For sure!!!

I look down at the message and take triple exclamation points as a sign of mild interest.

What are you thinking? she asks.

Erase Dylan from my mind, I want to type. That might sound odd. I consider what to do with her and glance at the tips of the Sandia mountains in the distance. I type in the first idea that comes to my head.

Want to go on a hike? I text back.

Can't wait!! she replies.

I slip my phone in my pocket and take a long, thankful breath, like someone just rescued me from a near drowning incident.

***

Three hours later, at practice, I watch Travis out of the corner of my eye. He's talking to one of the assistant coaches, his head leaned back and laughing. I imagine he's talking about Dylan and he's describing all the kinky positions they're going to practice in bed. I stretch my legs on the warm grass and try to block him out, but every time I hear him laugh I want to hurl a ball at his gloating head. Miles is sitting next to me, watching my expression fluctuate between annoyed, irate and fuming with vengeance.

"Dude, you alright?" Miles asks.

I don't answer him. I just shake my head. When Travis sits down in the grass and starts stretching, I pick myself up and grab my glove and a ball.

"Travis," I say as I walk towards him. He squints up at me and throws me a cocky grin. "I need to warm my arm up. You want to throw?" I ask.

"I should stretch first," he says and I pick his glove up off the ground and toss it in his hands.

"Thanks," I say. He hesitates for a second, but then he stands up. We walk towards the outfield and toss the ball back and forth. We start off with small talk and discuss our game this weekend in San Diego and some of the competition we're going to face. I pretend I care about other player's RBIs and batting averages.

Time to digress.

"I want you to stay away from Dylan," I say. It's not a question. It's not a subtle hint. It's a warning. I whip the ball hard and Travis catches it and smiles another cocky grin. He knew this was coming and, as always, he's more than happy to encourage a fight.

"I was just helping her out today," he says, all innocent.

"And you just happened to rub her leg?" I ask and match his casual tone. I throw another ball, a little bit harder. Travis catches it and the impact knocks his smile down a few pegs.

"Yeah, so? She's—" he pauses and flips the ball in his fingers as he thinks about this. "It's hard to describe her. She's cute, that's for sure." He gives me a second to let this observation sink it. It makes my teeth clench. "I'm thinking about asking her out," he says and whips the ball back at me and I catch it without taking my eyes off of his.

"I don't think so."

I throw the ball, lighter this time, and we keep tossing back and forth while Travis considers my words.

"You passed her up," he tells me. His words feel like he's taking a swing at me. "That makes her available."

I stare across the grass at him. "She's not interested in you. So don't waste your time." I know this advice is worthless. Nothing is out of Travis's league. A challenge only motivates him.

"I can change that," he says and smiles.

I stop throwing and fix my eyes on his. "Keep your hands off of her," I say slowly just to make sure I get my point across.

"I don't know if I can," he says and laughs a little. "I bet a girl like her is an animal in bed." Something like thunder rumbles through my body. I wind up and throw a curve ball high and as hard as I can and Travis barely has time to react to the throw. He blocks his forehead with his glove like a shield and the ball bounces off the leather with a loud smack. It knocks any trace of a grin off his face and sends him back pedaling a few steps. He throws his glove on the ground and stomps toward me.

"What's your problem?" he yells. Some of the guys warming up turn to watch us. I take a few quick steps until I'm in his face. All he needs is a good look at my eyes to know where I stand. I see the anger in his eyes settle as the truth sinks in.

"Oh," he says. He raises his eyebrows like he's surprised. And maybe he is. I'm sure he suspected I still liked Dylan. He didn't know I still loved her. "I get it," he says.

I stare him down a few seconds longer. "Thanks for the warm up," I say and walk away towards the infield. I feel like I'm in high school and I could win an immaturity award, but I don't care. Passing off Dylan as single is one thing. Exposing her to dickheads like Toolshed is another.

It really was the noble thing to do.

***

The next afternoon, I park in front of Kari's apartment. I stare up at the blue, two story house and feel guilty. What am I doing here? If I can't stand the thought of Dylan dating anyone, why do I get the privilege? But I would feel even worse if I canceled at the last second. So, I decide just to go through with it. Zero expectations.

I turn off the engine and get out of the car. It's a perfect day for hiking—seventy-five degrees and a clear blue sky. I take it as a good sign. I ring the doorbell and one of Kari's roommate's answers. She grins at me shyly and opens the door.

"Come on in," she says.

I walk into the living room and it smells like vanilla or cinnamon or something girly. There are white Christmas lights strewn all over the room even though it's almost May. The girl who opened the door introduces herself as Anna and another roommate sitting on the couch waves and tells me she's Kim. I say hi to both of them and Kari shouts that she'll be right out. I stand there and look at the walls and they're covered with framed nature photography. I think Dylan's pictures are better.

No I don't.

Damnit!! I swear that girl put some kind of a hex over my thought process.

When Kari walks into the living room I stare with surprise at what she's chosen to wear hiking: skinny jeans, platform flip flops, and a tank top that sparkles with rhinestones.

"Ready to go?" she asks.

I stare back at her. "Are you?"

"Oh, wait, let me grab my purse." She runs out of the room and her shoes clop with her down the hall. She's back in two seconds with a blue purse large enough to be a grocery bag hanging off her shoulder. She's smiling so huge and looks so excited that I feel awful. Maybe she forgot what we planned.

"What do you want to do?" I ask her.

"Don't you want to hike?" she asks.

"Um." Should I tell her to change into tennis shoes? Or is that rude?

I rub my hand over my stomach. Earlier this morning I had a bad feeling in my gut, but I couldn't decide if my gut was telling me I should back out of this date, or if it was hinting I should have used less hot sauce in my breakfast omelet. Now it's pretty obvious.

I play it safe. "You know, I don't really feel like hiking. We can do something else."

"No, let's hike. It'll be fun."

"Um, do you have tennis shoes?" I ask. You know, socks, shorts, sunglasses? Common hiking attire. I hear Kim laugh but she muffles it with a cough. I'm getting a sinking feeling in my chest.

"Oh, duh. Just a sec."

A half hour and two outfit changes later, Kari is ready to go. What I took for a laid-back girl majoring in sociology has ended up being a high-maintenance fashion diva that can't leave the house without her outfit carefully coordinated and approved by not one, but two roommate checks. Good, God. I'm so glad I'm not a girl.

I decide to take Kari to an easy trail called Rinconada Canyon loop on the outskirts of town. It's usually full of families and dogs. I figure if a six-year-old can hack it, she'll manage.

"I've never been on a hike before," Kari announces when I start the car.

No kidding.

"Really?" I say.

"I love the outdoors," she swoons. I glance down at her tennis shoes. They look like they've never seen the light of day. "It just takes so long to hike," she says. "It's like a full day event, when I can go to the gym and burn like five times as many calories in under an hour."

Like, you're totally right. I muffle a sigh. I am never taking Bubba's advice again.

We stop at Starbucks on the way to the park because Kari informs me she hasn't eaten all day. I wait for her to order a salad or a sandwich but all she wants is a large, soy, no foam, extra hot, sugar-free hazelnut latte with an extra shot. I'm amazed so many words can describe a single beverage. I offer to treat and stare in shock when the bill is over five dollars. Five bucks for coffee?? Freaking Starbucks. They should change their name to Fivebucks.

We pull up to a gravel parking lot next to the trail and dust kicks up around the tires. We park in front of an orange gate that marks the beginning of the trailhead. I promise Kari the path is really well marked, that it's a great beginner hike. She gets out of the car and looks around at the dusty parking lot with a frown. I meet her behind my car and she's staring down at her bright pink tennis shoes.

"I didn't think it would be so dirty out here."

I look down at her feet.

"It's just dust."

"I know, but these are my favorite shoes. They don't make this style anymore."

My mind shifts to Amanda. When we were in high school, we had a secret code we used when we needed to be saved from painful social situations. Our message was always: Pork chop sandwiches. I don't know why we called it that, or who started it, but it stuck as our emergency signal. I look up at the sky and think of pork chop sandwiches. I wonder if Amanda is looking down on us. Maybe she'll send a monsoon or dust storm our way to cut the date short. Sometimes I like to think she can still save me.

We start walking down the trail and Kari takes a long gulp of her latte. She complains the espresso shots taste burnt. I have no idea what she's talking about, but I nod and pretend to be sympathetic.

A half hour into the hike, things are only getting worse. Kari drank half her coffee and it's making her jumpy. There are a few flies buzzing around and she's constantly swatting the air in front of her face. She thinks she sees a Gila monster and screams, but I assure her it's just a gecko. She convinces herself that a vulture is stalking us.

"Do vultures attack humans?"

"I don't think so," I say. "Only in horror movies."

"Maybe it smells my coffee," she says.

I tell her she's safe. Vultures like good coffee, I joke. She glares at me. I switch tactics since she's too annoyed for humor and I try to be the encouraging hiking coach. When we pass a tight stretch of trail and her legs have to touch some of the tall grass, I commend her on her bravery. When she has to duck under a fallen tree limb and scale a few rock boulders, I tell her she's doing great. I pretend to be genuinely impressed by her adventurous tenacity.

I am so bored.

"Oh, my God, can scorpions fly?" she asks. I turn and stare back at her.

"What?"

"What is that thing?" She points down to a black bug crawling slowly across the trail.

I tell her it's a beetle.

"Ew, nasty. Will you kill it?"

I tell her to walk around it. "You can't kill bugs in nature. It's a rule."

"Gross." She quickly dances around it and shrieks at the same time. I commend her, once again, on being so daring. We keep walking and right now I'm more annoyed at Dylan than anyone. This is all her fault. I wouldn't be on this worthless date if I wasn't trying to get over her.

I hear Kari's feet stop dragging behind me and I glance at her over my shoulder. She's fixated on the scrubby bushes growing next to the path.

Is she delusional?

"Are you okay?" I ask.

She swallows and gasps. "Gray! I think there's a snake in these bushes. It's making a rattling noise." She presses a hand to her chest and freezes. I walk towards her and I don't hear a rattle, but then a grasshopper jumps out of the bushes and lands in her hair.

She screams and throws her coffee cup in the air. I feel like this is all happening in slow motion. Her coffee flies skyward, then flips into a skydive approach for her head. The cup misses her head, but hits her chest, releasing its contents of overpriced "burnt espresso" all over her tank top. She's screaming and flailing her arms and running in place like she's being attacked by a nest of wasps. I have to bite my lips together to keep a straight face.

I try to calm her down and keep yelling that it's just a grasshopper. An older couple scoots around us on the path and the guy raises his eyebrows at me. I see pity on his face.

I rest my hands on Kari's shoulders. She finally stops jumping and flailing and her terrified eyes meet mine. When she stops hyperventilating, I can't help it. I laugh. I laugh so hard I have to lean over.

"You thought a grasshopper was a rattlesnake," I say in between breaths.

And that's when she shoves me so hard she pushes me off the trail and I barely catch myself on a tree branch before I fall down the side of the cliff. After I find my balance and my minor heart attack subsides, I glare at her.

"Oh, that wasn't funny to you?" she says and her eyes turn from crybaby to psycho bitch in .2 seconds. She turns and stomps back down the trail, heading for the parking lot. I don't bother telling her the trail's a loop and it's just going to take longer going back the way we came. I'm still trying to calm down after my near brush with death.

I've just discovered that dating is not only detrimental to my budget, my patience and my rare free time. It's also threatening to my health. Good to know.

Dylan

Cat and I sit with Miles on his front porch. The three of us drink pink lemonade and eat potato chips and hamburgers. I have so many pickles it's giving me a stomach ache. Miles invited Cat over for lunch and Cat insisted I join them. It's the perfect spring afternoon—the temperature is mild and the sunlight is hitting the ground at just the right angle to make the trees and flowers shine like gold. Even though hiking with Gray would be my ideal scenario, I'm content to sit back and feel the breeze brush my skin.

I'm tapping my feet to the rhythm of Cat's guitar. The three of us are collaborating on a song we titled "Ode to Bacon." Miles and I write the lyrics while Cat improvises the chords. It's a beautiful moment in music discovery.

"It's still missing something," Cat says.

I rest my chin on my hand and concentrate. "I know. We need a verse dedicated to all the ways you can use bacon as a topping," I say.

"Didn't we already do that in the 'bacon as a condiment' verse?" Miles asks.

I lean back in my chair, thinking hard. "How about a verse dedicated to the flavor benefits of combining cheese with bacon?"

Cat crosses her legs and shakes her head. "I think that convolutes the message. We need to keep bacon in the spotlight. Cheese is a whole other song."

Miles informs Cat this song could really catapult her career.

"He's right," I say. "Cat, you should start practicing your Grammy acceptance speech."

The three of us are interrupted by a shout coming from the street, followed by someone slamming a car door shut.

"Kari, you're fine!"

It's Gray's voice and we all turn to see what's causing the commotion. A second later, a petite brunette in cut-off shorts and bright pink tennis shoes marches up the steps. Her white tank top is covered in brown stains. Her smooth hair is falling out of her ponytail. She's scratching at her legs, which are streaked with red splotches.

"Fine? My legs have poison oak all over them!"

Gray stumbles up the steps behind her and she turns to glower at him. Gray's face carries a plate of emotions: pissed off and guilty with a side of exhaustion. They don't notice the three of us sitting in the corner of the porch.

"It's not poison oak. I just think you had an allergic reaction—"

"And someone has precious baseball practice and can't take me to the emergency room," she says, her voice wavering.

Miles and I meet each other's eyes and he gives me this look like maybe we should step in and help out.

"Come on, I have some lotion you can use for the itching. You'll be fine."

Miles clears his throat and both of their eyes snap towards us. When Gray notices me, any trace of guilt on his face turns to pure rage.

"What are *you* doing here?" he asks me, specifically, but Miles answers him. He explains he invited us over for lunch and this, for some reason, annoys Gray even more.

What's his problem? Does everything I do piss him off?

"What happened to you?" Cat asks the girl.

Kari huffs. "Well, it's nice that someone here cares about my medical condition."

I watch Gray's face turn red and one of his hands locks into a fist. Kari bends down and runs her fingernails over her legs.

"Stop scratching. You're making it worse," Gray tells her.

"It hurts!"

"It wouldn't hurt if you'd stop scratching for two seconds."

"It's poison oak!"

"No, it's not," he yells back. I look back and forth between them and try to gauge whether this fight is mutual disgust or sexual tension. Gray reaches his hand out to touch Kari's shoulder in an attempt to calm her down, but she swats it away with a hard slap.

"Get your cheap hands off of me," she screams.

It's probably time to intervene, but I'm secretly enjoying the spectacle. I can't hangout with Toolshed, but Gray is free to waste a gorgeous afternoon on crybaby here?

"Cheap?" Gray asks.

"Yes. This is your white trash idea of a date? Hiking?"

"White trash?" Gray repeats. He looks more confused than angry.

Kari nods. "Very clever ploy, Gray. This way you get out of paying for anything."

He looks at the ground like there's a response written out on his feet.

"It's just a lame attempt to get out of spending money," Kari demands.

"I bought you coffee," he mumbles.

"Here's some advice, since you obviously need it," Kari shouts. "No woman actually likes hiking. Okay?"

"I love hiking," Cat says under her breath, but Kari doesn't hear her.

"And if they say they do, they're lying," Kari says. Miles, Cat and I exchange grins.

"We don't like camping and tents and bugs and sporting events," Kari insists.

"Hey," Miles speaks up. Apparently dissing sporting events is going too far.

I set my hand on his arm and stand up. I offer to get some cortisone for Kari. This reminds her of the stinging red blotches on her legs. Her mouth starts to tremble and she bends down and starts scratching at them again. My eyes flicker to Gray and he looks guilty.

"I think I'm having a severe reaction," she says. "I'm starting to feel nauseous."

"Probably because you slammed a gallon of coffee on an empty stomach," Gray says.

Before she can wind up and slap him again, I step between them. I offer to drive Kari to the emergency room if it would make her feel better. She sniffles and nods and Gray digs into his pockets and hands me his keys. His eyes meet mine and they barely look grateful. More than anything, he's furious. I get the sneaking suspicion it's my presence that's bothering him more than anything. It makes me feel sick to see this is how he reacts to me. That I'm such a burden for him to bear. It's making me doubt, again, what I'm doing here. The harder I try to knock down his walls, the higher he builds them.

Kari stomps down the steps and I follow her to Gray's car. I yell that I'll drop the keys off later. Gray's already disappeared into the house, the screen door slamming shut behind him. I turn and wave to Miles and Cat, who watch me with concern.

Gray

I'm lying on my bed, blaring *Missed the Boat,* by Modest Mouse. The lyrics seem appropriate considering my current disastrous dating karma. I've still got my practice shorts on and I'm icing my shoulder. I smell like sweat, my arm's sore, and I need to shower and write that stupid book review for Psych class. I pull my fingers through my hair and stare up at the ceiling. I feel terrible about Kari. Maybe I deserved to be called cheap. Maybe she's right, that I took her hiking so I wouldn't have to fork over sixty bucks for dinner with a girl I might not have chemistry with.

I hear a knock at my balcony door and I sigh at the ceiling. Speaking of chemistry…

A second later the door opens and Dylan crosses the room. I can feel her presence like heat, like sun rays touching my skin. My car keys land on my dresser with a clang. Out of the corner of my eye I see her turn, and I think she's going to walk right back out, but she sits down next to me on the bed. She props her elbow on my knee and her eyes study me, but I keep mine focused on a long, dark crack in the ceiling. It runs from one end of the room to the other. I wonder why the ceiling doesn't crash down and for a second I'm jealous. I wonder how you can be strong and hold yourself together with cracks stretching through your entire surface.

"Hey, you," she says.

I acknowledge her with a half grin. I love having her here on my bed. Her elbow resting on my knee. I hate that I love it.

"Kari's fine."

I blink at the ceiling.

"It wasn't poison oak," Dylan says. "You were right. It was just a reaction to field grass or something blooming on the path that brushed her leg. The doctor prescribed cortisone and Advil. She was hungry, so I treated her to Starbucks on the way home."

I squeeze the icepack harder against my shoulder and thank Dylan for taking her to the emergency room. I tell her I owe her one. She's quiet for a moment and I finally meet her eyes. There's a deep crease between them. She's upset about something.

"What is it?" I ask.

"Kari's not such a bad girl, you know. She was just scared today."

I shrug. I was scared too. It's not every day someone tries to push me off the side of a cliff.

"I don't think hiking is a white trash date idea," she adds.

I exhale loudly. "Give it a rest, Dylan."

"I'm just saying."

"It wasn't hiking," I say. I sit up on my elbows and stare at Dylan. "It was watching someone have a nervous breakdown for two hours straight. Her autobiography could be titled *Borderline Psychotic*." I flop back down on the bed and stare at the ceiling.

"I'm done," I say.

Dylan looks down at me. "Done?"

"With dating. It isn't worth it. It shouldn't be this painful."

"You're a little young to retire in the dating department."

"I suck at it." I rub my hand over my face. "It shouldn't be this much work."

Dylan shakes her head. "Not if it's the right person."

I can feel her eyes on me, but I refuse to meet her gaze. She sums up my entire dilemma in one sentence.

Dylan's voice softens. "Kari's really beautiful."

I smirk at this observation. "Beauty has its limits," I say. "Hers ends on the surface."

Dylan's quiet and she taps her feet to the music. She leans against my leg. It makes my whole body heat up. I have an urge to grab her arms and pull her on top of me. I clench my fingers tighter around the ice pack instead.

"So, is Kari your type these days?" Dylan asks.

"What do you mean?" I ask.

"You know, petite, big boobs, wears short-shorts."

I narrow my eyes at this question and I know what Dylan's getting at. All of those features are the exact opposite of her, like I'm trying to avoid every aspect of Dylan. Find her complete opposite. Stay the furthest away from her that I can. In a way, maybe I am.

"I don't have a type."

Dylan's hair falls over her shoulder and brushes the skin on my chest and it makes my stomach tense up. I glance at her but she's oblivious to her affect on me. She's looking away from me, absorbed in her thoughts. I touch some of her hair and it feels light and warm, like silk.

Maybe that's why I'm so attracted to Dylan. She's so unaware. She doesn't even try to catch my attention. She doesn't try to be sexy or force herself to look just right. She just is. And it makes me crave her that much more, because she hides all of that sexiness under the surface. It's more of a challenge to pull it out.

I curl my fingers around her wrist and she looks down at me.

"You know why I asked Kari out, don't you?"

She raises a single shoulder. "Because you like her?"

I close my eyes and shake my head. "I'm trying to avoid you." I'm surprised to hear myself admit it out loud.

Dylan pulls her arm out of my grasp and leans away from me. "I get it, Gray," she says. "You're over me. Congratulations. But you could at least be honest with me. You could have told me you had a date today."

I look up at her. "You believe I'm over you?" I ask. Did I fool one of the most perceptive girls I've ever met?

She says it's obvious. "You should see the way you look at me sometimes. Like you despise me. Like it makes your skin crawl to be in the same room with me. I hate that I have that effect on you." She looks down at the empty space between us. "You were right. I waited too long and I'm trying to bring the past back instead of just accepting this is over."

I feel my chest ache. Finally, all this acting paid off. Then why do I feel sick about it? Maybe I wanted to hurt her, because she hurt me. I wanted her to see what it's like to feel powerless. To love somebody and lose them.

Her eyes meet mine and they're filled with sadness. This has gone on too long. It's time to stop thinking so hard and move.

I sit up and grab her face in my hands and kiss her. The ice pack slides between us and it's wet against my chest. Even though my shoulder's numb, when she touches it, her fingers burn my skin.

It's just a kiss, I remind myself. That's all.

I lean back and pull her on top of me. Her hair falls all around us and I have to brush it away. The ice pack crunches between us and I grab it and throw it on the floor. I wrap her in my arms and I feel like I'm holding layers of happiness.

It's just one kiss.

I drink in her mouth and taste her tongue and my mind is a rollercoaster. My heart pulls apart and collides back together with so much force that my hands start to shake. I feel like I'm speeding down a highway in the middle of the night with no headlights turned on.

A single kiss can be one of the craziest things you ever do.

***

I stare up at my bedroom ceiling after she leaves and replay the kiss over and over in my head like a song on repeat and I taste it and savor it until my stomach flips so many times it hurts.

I learned something tonight. Love always finds you, no matter how hard you try to avoid it. It knows your hiding places. It's smarter that you'll ever be.

And love is patient. It waits. Sometimes it waits until you give up. Just to prove you wrong.

But sometimes I'd rather hide than feel this way because when I'm with her the chemical reaction is too strong. Sparks shoot off behind my eyes. It's my own free firework show. But I don't know if I want it. Fireworks scared me when I was a kid—the ashes falling from the sky, the screaming spectators, the flashing streaks of light and noise you could feel jostle the ground.

I imagined the fireworks could hit the stars. Could shatter something whole. That the lights could fall on me like boulders, crushing me.

That's how you make me feel tonight. You. Crush.
Me. Under your magnificent light show.

Dylan

Gray once told me he thinks musicians are the greatest magicians. Sometimes that's the way I feel about photography. It feels like magic, to be able to capture an entire mountain and hold it inside a tiny frame. To be able to take the sky-line of New York City, with all of its lights, or the city of Prague with its tunnel of bridges and compress it neatly on a single print. Cameras give one person a thousand eyes. They take us light years away. Pictures introduce us to a million strangers. They let us travel to other planets. It's like teleporting. It's the magic that intrigues me.

My first gallery show is a small turnout of dedicated regulars. I showcase twenty pictures and over the course of four hours about twenty people come and go. I end up selling eight prints.

I listen to people analyze my photographs all evening. They call my vision fresh. Innovative. People ask what inspires me. Is it my fascination with emotions? Is it to reveal our humanity? Is it to show people wear the same expressions, whether we're young or old?

Really, I don't think about it. I don't plan my photos in advance; I don't try and predict what people will do. I never stage a shot. It's more fun to be surprised. Life's a better story if you let it unfold naturally. When you force it, things become a chore because you close yourself off to possibility. You experience the most when you're not looking for anything in particular. Photography is the same way.

By the end of the show I'm giddy and exhausted and my feet hurt from wearing new sandals. Liz, (my fashion tutor), helped me coordinate the look of an aspiring photographer. She paired my knee-length turquoise skirt with a simple, brown tank top and leather belt, hanging low on my waist, with small amber and turquoise beads sewn around the buckle. It's a little too color-coordinated for my taste, but Liz says my complexion works best with earth tones, whatever that means.

When the last customer leaves, Barb begins stacking dishes on the table next to the empty vegetable and cheese spreads.

"I think you found your calling," Barb said. "Selling eight pieces is great for a first show. It's all about networking from here." She's right, because even people that didn't buy my photos were still interested in my work. One woman hired me do a landscape series of her property. A man hired me to photograph his Bernese Mountain Dogs. I set up two photo shoots for the following week. The word was starting to spread.

Barb tells me she has some book-keeping to do and asks me to lock the door on my way out. She disappears down the hall. I pick up a stack of flyers I printed to advertise my photography and lean down to stuff them in my backpack. Someone clears their throat.

I look up, and Gray is leaning in the doorway, decked out in his baseball uniform. He stands with one arm at his side and the other behind his back.

"Hey, you," he says and smiles. His skin is flushed, his hair is all messy and his eyes are bright. There's dirt all over his chest and up the side of one leg. Seeing him in his uniform makes me want to do one thing. Rip it off. He's standing there all normal like I should be expecting him to show up in his game clothes.

"Hi," I say, standing up.

He glances down at my outfit and walks towards me. His face is glistening with sweat. It looks like he sprinted here after the game.

"Congratulations on your first show," he says and from behind his back he pulls out a handful of my favorite flower, Birds of Paradise.

I reach out and trace their bright orange petals with my fingers. I take the bouquet carefully, like he gave me a rainbow and I don't want to disrupt the beauty of it.

He looks around at the empty room. "Sorry I missed it," he says.

"Sorry I missed your game," I say.

"No you're not," he says. "You don't have the attention span for baseball."

I've only been to one of his games. Until a week ago I thought he'd throw a ball at my head if he caught sight of me in the stands. I sat with Liz and tried to concentrate, but by the fourth inning I couldn't sit still and spent the rest of the game playing sports photographer.

"It could just use a few more exciting features."

His eyes slide down my body. "Like what?"

A few sexual ideas come to mind.

I clear my throat. "Well," I say. "First, I would change the uniform. You would all play in boxer briefs."

"Nice," he says. "I'm sure our mostly male fans would respond very well to that."

"And there would only be four innings."

"Four?"

"And each batter gets one ball and one strike. That's it. The pitcher would have to throw the ball through a flaming circle of fire. And after every game there'd be a firework show, followed by a team strip dance."

He just smiles, one of those lazy smiles that completes my day.

"I wouldn't recommend going into sports marketing, not to kill your life ambitions," he says. He walks around the room and studies my pictures and I just study him. He should look out of place wearing a baseball uniform in an art gallery, but it just makes him look more masculine. He's still wearing his cleats and they tap on the wood floor.

"These are really good," he says. "You're so good at seeing people."

"It's not that hard," I say.

Gray asks me about a few of the pictures and I point out my favorites. Then he turns to me. He's so close I can smell dirt and sweat, but mostly just him. He leans in closer until his forehead is touching mine.

"I didn't really come here to see your photos," he says.

"You didn't?"

He shakes his head and leans away so he can look in my eyes. He slowly brushes the hair off my shoulders. He takes his time. First one side. Then the other.

"I wanted to see you in a skirt," he says with another lazy grin. He runs his fingers down my neck and chest, until they land at my waist. I try to swallow or think but all I can do is feel the trail of his hands. He pulls me closer and closes his eyes and I think he's about to kiss me so I close mine. But he stalls and then his lips are against my ear.

"You know I love you, right?"

His breathing gives me the chills. Or maybe it's the words I've been waiting to hear for months.

Gray

When I drop Dylan off, we both hesitate. We know what will happen if I go inside.

Everything will change.

I turn down my stereo, but neither of us says anything. She picks up her bag and gently lifts the flowers off her lap when she opens the door. I know she's waiting for me to make the call. She leans over and kisses my lips. She takes her time pulling away. She says goodnight and I watch her walk up the cobblestone path to her apartment door.

She closes the door and I panic. What the hell am I waiting for? A written invitation? There's no reason to hold back now.

Because everything already has changed.

I turn off the engine, grab a CD, and get out of the car. I cross the driveway and open the door without knocking. Dylan's sitting on the bed with her legs crossed. She was expecting me. She's already stripped down to her underwear. It's a black, matching set.

She unleashes one of her killer smiles at me and it makes me freeze. She's the sexiest angel on earth. I lean against the door until it clicks shut, and walk over to the stereo to put in my CD.

"It's Ryan Adams' new album," I tell her. "I thought we could turn off the lights and listen to it. Naked." I stand up and start to un-do the buttons of my uniform.

"Wait," she says. "I really want to do that."

She walks over to me and I wrap my arms low around her waist and when I discover she's wearing a thong, my fingers dig into her skin. I pull our hips together. All the blood in my body rushes to one place with so much force it makes me shudder. I unbutton her bra with the first try and slip it off, but she hasn't even managed to undo one button yet.

"I hate these things," she mumbles and I graze my lips across hers. "Can't they snap off?" she says.

"Or be Velcro," I offer as I undo a couple buttons for her. She leans her head away from me.

"That's brilliant," she says. "That's what we need to invent. Dresses and shirts and pants that can be ripped off in one swift motion."

She looks at me expectantly, like I'm going to stop everything and agree to patent her new fashion line idea. Instead, I lean into her neck.

"We can call the brand 'easy access,'" she says. "We'll make millions."

"Dylan," I say, and look into her eyes, two inches away from mine. "Shut up." I lift her up and carry her over to the bed, keeping my lips suctioned to hers because even though I love hearing her strange ideas, I'm not in the mood to talk.

For the first time in six months, my head is clear. The world is set right again. Happiness is flooding through me. I feel like I'm back. It's me again. I'm whole. All the drama deflates because, finally, I'm smart enough to let go.

Dylan

I meet Gray on campus the next afternoon at the bottom of the Union steps and he throws an arm around me. It feels normal, like this has always been our routine, like I meet him on campus every afternoon and we grab lunch and reminisce about our completely amazing sex life.

"I have a few hours before practice," he says. "What do you want to do?" He kisses my neck and I wrap my fingers in his. We start walking down the sidewalk and his fingers play around inside mine, feeling and squeezing. I'm not a fan of public displays of affection, but I can't keep my hands off of Gray. Especially when he wears his baseball cap backwards so his eyes are in full view and his arm is tight around me.

"Let's do something nice for somebody," I say.

"Why?" he asks. People pass by and I can tell by their double takes that they recognize him, but he's oblivious.

"What do you mean why? Because you should always do things for other people," I say and lean against him.

"Why don't you do something nice for *me*? Like take me back to your place and get me naked?"

I grin as he runs his hand up my waist. "Get your brain out of your pants."

He nods to a few guys that say hi to him and I watch a group of girls pass and narrow their eyes in my direction. I smile back at them.

"What is it with you and helping people?" he asks as we weave around a few students on skateboards.

"I try to do one nice thing a day for somebody else."

"Give me a break," he says.

We pass an open courtyard, surrounded by campus buildings. In the center is a carpet of grass, crowded with students laying out and eating lunch. We sit down on a bench and watch a man wearing cut-off jean shorts juggle three sticks in the middle of the courtyard.

"Okay, fine," Gray says. "Let's do something nice for somebody. How about we buy that juggler some shorts that actually fit? No man should reveal that much thigh to the world."

I look at the man's skinny legs and point out he has nice thighs. Gray responds by running his hand up my own leg until it's resting on the inside of my thigh. He slowly glides his hand up until I pull it away. I stare at his grin with fascination. I wonder if I'll ever get used to his smile.

"So, what's your idea?" he asks me. I tell Gray it depends on the person.

"Sometimes I'll close my eyes and point to someone's name in the phonebook and write them a 'thinking of you' card. We could do that."

"That gesture's a little more creepy than nice," he points out.

"Come on, isn't there someone you know that could use a favor?" I ask him. He looks at me and his eyes turn thoughtful because he can tell I'm serious. He turns to study the buildings in front of us and I think he's going to throw me another sarcastic comment, but he stands and pulls me up next to him.

"I know who we can help," he tells me. We cross the courtyard and head towards an office building with a sign that says "Admissions."

Gray

Three hours later, we head to the Brew House with a stack of papers. Dylan has me go in alone, so Lenny doesn't feel like we're ganging up on her. When I walk in, I find Lenny sitting in the back of the restaurant going over some paperwork. She offers me a grim smile when she sees me, one that looks forced. I study her solemn expression and for the first time, I realize she always looks like this. Unhappy. Frustrated. Pissed off at the world. Maybe I never saw it before because that's how I felt. I was so unhappy I didn't even notice. My throat starts to get tight. I should have done this for Lenny months ago. I hate it that Dylan's always right, as if she holds life and people and friends under a magnifying glass for me, so I see everything clearly. Why can't I learn to see these things on my own?

"Hey," I say. She raises an eyebrow at me. "I have a surprise for you."

I sit down across from her and set a pile of papers on the table between us.

"Wow," she says. "Thanks. I've always wanted your class notes."

"They're applications, smartass, to fill out so you can start school in the fall. You might even be able to take summer school if you register soon enough."

She examines the papers with a frown. She pushes them back at me, as if I just offered her food she's allergic to. She says it's a nice thought but it's not going to happen.

I'm not giving up that easy. "I talked to an advisor. She can help you figure out all the classes you'll need for the nursing program. She gave me her card." I take the business card out of my pocket and set it on the pile. Lenny picks it up. For an instant she looks curious, but then she shakes her head and sets the card down.

"I don't think so. Thanks anyway." She blows me off and focuses back on the binder she was working on. Why did I have to pick the most stubborn person in Albuquerque to try and help? I shove her binder to edge of the table.

"What's your problem?" she says.

"What's your problem? Why won't you at least try?" I ask. "Are you worried you won't get in?" I ask.

"No," Lenny shoots back. "I was already accepted two years ago. I never registered for classes because unlike most of the spoiled brats at this school, mom and dad can't pay for my education. I don't get a go-to-college-for-free credit card. In fact, mom borrows money from me half the time to help pay rent. Get it? I can't go to school *and* work full time."

I narrow my eyes at her. "A lot of people go to school without any help. It's called student loans. And maybe you can work part time during school."

Lenny shakes her head. "It won't work. But thanks for trying. Really."

I tap my foot against the ground and try to read what she's thinking. "Why are you so afraid of doing something for yourself?" I ask.

"Excuse me?"

I look around the café. "You hate this job. You complain about it every single day. So, why are you wasting your time? What are you afraid of?"

Lenny frowns. "Dylan put you up to this, didn't she?" Before I answer she leans over the table and lashes out at me. "Well not everyone's as ballsy as Dylan, okay? My mom would shit a brick if she found out I left a full time management position, with benefits and a salary, to go back to school and rack up student loans. My parents didn't go to college. They don't understand. My mom didn't even graduate from high school. And Dad isn't much help, since we haven't heard from him in six months. I'm the only thing holding us together right now."

This is so strange, to hear these words. To listen to Lenny's situation. She's in the same dilemma I was in back in Phoenix. Feeling responsible. Stuck. Seeing no way out until someone believes in you, forces you to have the courage to change. But I was never selfless enough to help Lenny. I was too busy feeling sorry for myself.

"I bet your mom wants you to be happy," I say.

Lenny takes a deep breath. "She also wants to be able to pay the electricity bill. I can't afford school right now. We're broke."

I tap my fingers on the table. "What if somebody paid for you to go to school?"

She stares at me. "What are you saying, Gray? You're going to hook me up with a sugar daddy? Is there some 'sex for school' program I'm unaware of?"

I smile back at her. Just like me, she turns something serious into a joke when she doesn't want to face it. "I'm saying you can apply for a scholarship. If someone paid for you to go to school, would your mom be happier about it?"

Lenny shakes her head. "I'm not going to get a scholarship. I don't play sports and I wasn't a valedictorian of my high school."

"You're missing something obvious here," I say.

"What? Is there a scholarship available for disgruntled food industry workers?"

Dylan pointed this out to me at the admissions office and it never even occurred to me, but it's perfect. It's Lenny's chance.

I still have a few papers in my hand and I throw them on the table. "Just read them over, that's all I ask."

She picks up the papers. "What are these?"

"Every year they offer full-ride scholarships for minority students. You're also really smart and an over-achiever. You have a great shot at getting one of these scholarships."

She stares down at the papers. "How did you find these?"

"We did some research."

She stares back at me. "We?"

"Okay, maybe Dylan pressed this."

Her mouth twitches. She's almost smiling and for Lenny, that's a breakthrough.

"I also wrote you a letter of recommendation." I ruffle through the pile and pull out the letter that Dylan and I threw together at an extra computer in the admissions office. She picks it up and starts to read it and her mouth trembles. Oh, my God, I cannot handle seeing Lenny cry. No way. She looks up at me and there are tears in her eyes, but I pretend I don't notice. We don't do sentimental stuff. I stick to business because I know Lenny would rather vomit than do the sappy cry-in-my-arms hug.

"You need two more letters of recommendation," I say. "I also scheduled a time for you to meet with that advisor." She shakes her head because I know her schedule as well as she does. I point out the time on the back of the business card.

"Thanks."

I stand up, but before I leave, I add one more thing. A sincere regret. "Sorry I didn't do this for you sooner."

She smiles.

I head out the door and Dylan's down the street waiting for me. She's taking a picture of something on the ground that's invisible to the average eye. She's sprawled on the sidewalk and I remember the first day we met—that dusty courtyard in Phoenix, and I think how incredible it is that a single person can change your life. I'll do anything for her now. Anything. She helps people become twice their potential. She deserves the same thing in return.

Gray

We're all eating dinner Sunday night and Dylan's sitting across from me. I notice how, lately, her outfits all match and fit her. I have to admit, she looks good. The clothes show off her body and she can pull off anything because she's so tall and wiry. But it's also a little disappointing, because suddenly Dylan is fitting in. The change makes me feel unsettled because in the back of my mind, I know it's me that she's trying to please.

Over dinner, Liz is discussing wedding plans and all the guys nod politely like we care. She suggests Dylan look into doing wedding photography in Albuquerque this summer.

"It's really good money. We're paying a photographer three hundred dollars for two hours of work," she says.

"I'd love it," Dylan says. "But I won't be here this summer."

I already know this. Dylan has restless cells and they lose their shimmer if she's too stagnant. The rest of the table is stunned. In their eyes, Dylan's life is here. Settled. Next comes routine.

"Where are you going?" Travis asks.

Dylan explains she's been a kayaking instructor for the past few years in Northern Wisconsin. She guides trips through sea caves in Lake Superior, and leads camping trips in the Apostle Islands. Her eyes light up while she talks about it. She says it's the best way to spend the summer, that she's paid to watch the sunset over the Great Lakes. She can't pass it up.

"So it's just a summer thing? You're coming back here next fall, right?" Liz presses.

"Of course you are," Cat finishes. "I promise not to raise your rent."

I wait for the words. Here they come. Any second now.

"I wasn't planning on living here next fall."

I listen for a fork to drop. Someone to gasp. Choke. At least a beverage to get knocked over by a shaky hand. But it's just dead silence.

I look across the table at Dylan. The eclipse is just beginning to start.

"Why not?" Miles asks and his eyes quickly flicker to mine. He's gauging my reaction, but I'm already prepared for all this. All along I've known I'll have to let her go because I understand her better than anyone.

Dylan shrugs. "I just hadn't planned on staying here permanently," she says. She sets down her glass and her eyes skitter over all of the faces staring in her direction. Even Dylan can get nervous being center stage. "I'm a traveler," she says, like it's simple, like we should accept her and leave her alone about it. Dylan never judges a soul; she never questions people's motives or choices. She's the most open minded person I've ever met, yet everyone loves to judge her.

"You're a traveler?" Travis says. "What does that mean?"

Dylan extends her arms out wide. "It's a big world. I think life expands in proportion to how open you are to it.

I want to experience as much as I can. Especially while I'm young. Now's the time to do it."

"Well, you've gone to all this trouble to get your photography business started," Todd says. "It's just taking off. It's a pretty stupid career move if you ask me."

"Photography isn't my job. I'm not looking for a career right now."

"But you're really talented," Bubba says. I'm impressed to hear him compliment someone. Even thick-shelled Bubba has a soft spot for Dylan.

"I love it," Dylan says. "But it's not what defines me. I don't want anything to define me."

"Do you have something against Albuquerque?" Liz asks.

"What about Gray?" Lenny presses. I shoot Lenny a warning look.

"What about your friends?" Cat asks. "Don't you want to come back here?"

"What are you running away from?" Todd adds.

"Why can't you just stay in one place and make the most of it?" Travis demands.

Dylan raises her hands out like she's trying to block their words with a shield.

"Just, listen. I'm not running away. I'm sorry. I love you all. You've made this an unforgettable time and I'll definitely be back to visit, but I never planned on living here."

"Why not?" Liz demands.

I stare at Dylan. Explain yourself. Explain why permanence scares you so much.

"Look, you all have passions that motivate you. You're all pursuing your own things. You have baseball or school or jobs. Well, I have this calling to move around and to meet people. It's what inspires me. That's the best way I can explain it."

Her perfect mouth falls into a frown. For a tiny instant, I see her wither. And it hurts me to see it because she's more amazing than anyone I've ever met. She'll go further than any of us. She has a capacity to love more than all of us combined. That's why I know she'll bounce back. She has to. She'll follow her heart before she lets a stampede of opinions knock her down.

***

After dinner, Dylan follows me up to my room. She knows I have to study so she picks up her backpack and leans over me to give me a kiss goodnight. I'm not letting her go that easy. I pull her up onto the bed with me until she's in my lap and I lean against the wall and hold her close because I feel the need to protect her. Maybe Dylan's right. People love her and crave and need her, but so few understand her.

"What's wrong?" I ask. She's been quiet since dinner. Reflective. Self-conscious. It's making me feel guilty, like I'm the one that's responsible. I brush her hair back so I can see her face.

"I hate talking about myself."

"Too bad." I shift her on my lap so she's facing me.

"I don't even like thinking about myself. It's a waste of time."

"You have to think about yourself once in a while."

She thinks about this. "Why?"

"Because people will walk all over you if you don't. Come on, Dylan. You can sit and analyze a cloud for an hour, and you can't even tell me what's wrong?"

She looks up at my ceiling as if there's a sky above us.

"It's the dinner conversation," I say, since she's being too stubborn to bring it up.

"Dinner attack is more like it. It came from all sides. These blasts of questions. It was like a public stoning." She takes a deep breath and focuses on me. "Am I selfish, Gray?"

I shake my head. "Who cares what other people think? Don't let other people's opinions make you second guess what's important to you. You can't make everybody happy, believe me."

"That doesn't answer my question."

I take my time answering. "I think you're the most unselfish person I've ever met."

"Really?"

"Dylan, they don't know you. Let it go."

"Why am I so hard to understand?"

I rub my fingers down her bare arm as I think about this. Oh, man, how do I describe her?

"You're an abnormality. People get scared when they come across something that doesn't behave the way they expect it to. People like labels and categories and things they can predict. When people can't explain something, they assume it's because there's something wrong with it. They try to fix it or change it. They mess with it until it's translatable and they bring it down to their level. Trying to change someone is easier than trying to accept them. It's how we're programmed."

"Nice theory," she says. She leans her head on my shoulder, takes off my hat and runs her fingers through my hair. I look at her and wish I could wipe all her doubts away, like an eraser cleaning off a blackboard crammed full of questions. She runs her finger down my nose and over my lips. "But you're not like that."

I shrug. "If you can't accept people the way they are, I say step aside and leave them alone. Nobody gives each other a break anymore. People are so uptight."

I squeeze my arms tighter around her. I love this girl so much. Her energy can be a shock to the system and sometimes you need a little time to acclimate, but when you're next to her, your body soars at a higher altitude, the air becomes thinner and your heart beats faster. We need more Dylan's. People like her are the artists and painters and dreamers. They make the world move and shake and they take a life that's mundane and bland and color it in. That's why I'll never let her change.

Dylan

"Think about it, Dylan," Liz says. "You have everything going for you here, right now." I'm sitting at the Brew House with Cat and Liz. Lenny sat down to join us for a few minutes. "There's a fine line between being adventurous and being stupid. Don't pass up a perfect life that's right in front of you just because you're too far-sighted to see it," she says.

I listen to their opinions. I'm used to it. Everyone seems to have opinions about my choices. They're still determined to give me a hard time and I know they're doing it because they care about me. And they care about Gray. So I drink my coffee and I nod my head. Some of their logic starts to sink in.

"You've got love," Cat says. "True love. What else do you need? What else is there to live for?"

"Don't say crap like that around me," Lenny says. "You're going to make me gag."

"I'm worried about you," Liz says.

I stare back at her. "Why are you worried about me?"

"I get that you're a free spirit," she says. "And that's cool, but it gets old. Life doesn't get much better than what you have in front of you right now, and if you leave, you're going to look back someday and regret it."

"Relationships aren't like library books," Cat adds. "You can't just check people in and out whenever you feel like it."

Her words hurt because they're true.

"I think you're being selfish," Liz says.

I feel my heart wince. I think back to what Gray says. *They don't know you.*

"Why did you come to Albuquerque?" Cat reminds me. "What's the number one reason?"

"To see Gray."

"Why?"

"He's my soulmate and future husband," I say, repeating what I had said to her in Switzerland.

"I think you only love him when it's convenient for you," Liz says.

"What do you guys want from me?" I plead. "I came back here. I'm trying to set things right with Gray. I'm never going to hurt him again."

"Then why don't you come back next fall?" Cat asks. "You have a place to live. You can work on your photography. You can work in Wisconsin during the summers or travel while Gray's away playing baseball. That way everybody wins. Gray doesn't get hurt. You two stay together. Isn't that what you want?"

I digest their thoughts and their words and try to piece it all together and it all starts to make sense. I always thought love would be easy and slip into place when the moment is right. But, how far do you go for love? How much of your life do you give up for a single person? And how much do you let yourself change? When you stop being yourself, who will you become?

Gray

When you finally let down your walls, it's amazing how much sunlight pours through. When you stop worrying so much about your life, you suddenly start living it. This state of mind makes me want to blare power ballads from my car speakers. I even bought *Heart's* greatest hits. Never shop for music under the influence of love. It's embarrassing what you're in the mood for.

Dylan and I are together whenever humanly possible. My world is perfect. Until something isn't right.

I start to notice more changes about her. At first it was just her clothes. But something else has changed. Her eyes look a little faded, like a light has crawled out from inside of them, like she's tired. Except I know it isn't a lack of sleep. It's a lack of adventure. A lack of movement. There's a slower gait to her walk. Her hands are calm, usually clasped over her lap as if this will slow her down. She's a little quieter too. Not as many dares. Not nearly as many random thoughts.

Today I notice the strangest change of all. I played an afternoon game, so I take Dylan out for dinner in Old Town. It's an old-fashioned Spanish pueblo in the middle of the city. The small buildings have adobe-style architecture with flat roofs and curved edges, the stucco walls brushed smooth to look like soft, tan suede. A church is anchored in the middle of the square, surrounded by an open, central plaza. Dylan and I sit at an outdoor patio that overlooks the plaza and we eat enchiladas with red and green chile salsa.

It's a perfect night. But something's missing. I look around us and finally I pinpoint the problem.

"Where's your best friend?" I ask Dylan.

Dylan points at me, because I'm obviously sitting across from her.

"Your camera," I say. "I thought it was surgically attached to you. Where is it?"

"I left it at home."

I set down my fork and study her like she's crazy. "Can you even see without it? I've never seen you step outside your door without your camera."

"It's not that big of a deal," she says. She looks away from me, her eyes measuring something in the courtyard. I can tell she wants to take a picture. The sunset is going to be incredible, with so many feathery clouds in the sky. She rubs her arms and I notice her eyes are sad. Sad.

"Spill it."

She hangs her head a little bit. "This might sound stupid, but I'm afraid I'll use up all my photo opportunities."

"What? How would that ever happen?"

"Well, I decided to take Cat's offer. I'm coming back here next fall."

I hear the words come out, but I don't believe it. "You want to come back here?"

She nods.

"To live?" I say with shock. She nods again.

"Haven't you thought about it?" she asks.

I look down at my plate. I've thought about it hundreds of times. But I gave up on the idea last summer, when she shot it down in Phoenix.

"What about your dream list? Backpacking in Australia and living in a big city and traveling in Central America?"

She smiles. "I also added Singapore and Hong Kong to the list."

"So, you're just going to give that all up?"

"I want you to be happy," she says.

"I want you to be happy," I argue.

"Maybe I outgrew my dreams," she says. "Maybe dreams change based on the people you meet and the places you go. I can make new dreams, ones that include you."

I turn and watch a family pass us on the sidewalk. I'm starting to lose my appetite. I test her. I ask her what random thing she did today.

She smirks. "I browsed a class schedule for next fall."

This is too much. "What? I thought you hated college," I argue.

"I never said I hated it. I'm just against the overall philosophy of institutionalized education."

I lean over the table and press my hand against her forehead, like I'm checking for a fever. "Dylan, do we need to perform an exorcism? Has some evil college-rearing demon possessed your soul?"

She pulls back. "Isn't it normal to want to go to college?"

"Since when do you care about doing normal things?"

She sighs and finally gives in. She tells me Miles hinted that if she's going to come back next fall, she should look into to taking some classes while she's out here. Then, she looks at me like what she's about to say is insane. Like I should prepare myself.

"I'm also going to be in a book club with Liz," she announces.

"A book club? Since when do you have the patience to read a book?"

She crosses her arms over her chest. "I read sometimes."

"Sometimes? You can barely get through a menu without being distracted. It's one of your best qualities."

She ignores the compliment. "Well, maybe it's time to work on my attention span. And Cat offered to hire me part time to work on promotions for her band."

Dylan smiles, but I frown. "Promotions?"

"Yeah, like help her schedule shows and find venues to play at." Since when is Dylan organized? "And Travis wants to hire me to take some photos for his fan page."

I shake my head at this ridiculous job offer. Only Toolshed has his own college fan website and sports blog.

"Lenny even offered to give me cooking lessons, since we'll stick to our Sunday night dinner schedule."

I narrow my eyes. I know exactly what Liz and Cat and Miles and Travis are doing. Even Lenny. They're trying to keep her here. Lock her down. Cut her wings. Make sure that she's tied down with school and jobs and clubs and all the things Dylan has never been remotely interested in. They want to anchor her here. But don't they get that she's a sail?

"That doesn't sound like you."

Her chin is held high. "It is me."

I need to know. "Since when do you care what other people think?"

Dylan doesn't hesitate. "I don't care what they think, Gray. But I care what you think."

"Why?" I ask.

"Because I love you. And I know if I leave I'll just hurt you again. I can't do that."

Her face is stubborn. She's staying.

"Don't do it for me. I just want you to be yourself."

"But when I try to be that person, I end up hurting you."

I shake my head. "You're perfect," I say.

I should be happy. My dreams are all coming true. But at a cost I can't afford. I know better. I see this angel sinking down to the ground only to get dust on her wings, only to shine less because she's meant to live so much wider than this confined life. All for me.

Gray

Mom and Dad get in on Friday to stay for the weekend. One of the strangest things about leaving home is having your parents come to visit you in your new domain. It's a role reversal because suddenly they're standing in your home and they have to ask your permission to turn on the television or park in the driveway or eat something out of the fridge and you have to lay down the rules.

Conversation becomes a careful balance. You won't fill them in on too much of your love life (because really, do they want to hear about it?), you don't tell them too much about your social life (they were in college once; they know the scene), and you certainly don't fill them in on your problems (guess what, I was a stoner for the past six months!). You keep your talks centered around school and sports and the general weather in your area. You don't want to act homesick, because they'll get these worry wrinkles on their foreheads. Yet, you also don't want to seem too ecstatic to be free from their hovering control; you'll just make them feel bad. So, you tell them you're happy and you like school, but you sure do miss mom's cooking and dad's brilliant sports analysis. Everyone's satisfied. You win a gold star every time.

Your relationship turns into one long shopping list. They take you out and buy you things so they feel needed, like they still cover you with their umbrella of love and protection and you're still their baby. You humbly regress into the dependent adolescent that, well, you are, and thank them for the groceries, the dinners out, the toiletries, cleaning products and new underwear and socks. They buy all the necessary, boring stuff that you would never waste your money on because you can't possibly cut into your entertainment budget for something as lame as floss.

I haven't seen my parents since winter break. The first thing my mom wants to do when they stop by is inspect our kitchen cupboards and the first thing my dad wants to do is sit down and discuss my season in detail. I stand against the kitchen counter and study them.

The big question is, do I ask Dylan to meet them? She met my mom briefly in Phoenix, but it was before we were anything and now we're sort of something, maybe. How do I explain this to my parents? Hey, mom and dad, meet my on-again, off-again best friend, semi-girlfriend, sex partner, but most-likely-this-will-end-very-badly, spring fling, Dylan.

"How's your arm feeling?" Mom asks.

"Do you think it's too late for me to get a tee time tomorrow morning? You wouldn't be interested in playing a round, would you?" Dad asks.

"Honey, what Gray needs are groceries."

"Clair, he's old enough to buy his own groceries."

"Your kitchen smells a little funky, Gray," Mom observes. Do all moms have an acute sense of smell or is it just mine? "Have you given the sink a good scrub lately?"

I wonder to myself if we even own a scrubbing utensil.

She opens the pantry door and shakes her head at our messily arranged boxes of processed food. "Gray, do you take a multi-vitamin?"

"Yankees and Red Sox are playing tomorrow afternoon," Dad points out.

"Oh, is that all we're going to do this weekend? Watch baseball?" Mom complains.

"You can take the car downtown whenever you want," he reminds her.

"I don't know dear, Albuquerque has a lot of crime. I don't want to go out by myself. Gray, should we get you a club for your car?"

My dad picks up the newspaper he has tucked under his arm and starts browsing the sports section. "No one's going to steal a ten-year-old hatchback, Clair."

"Is your neighborhood safe, Gray? You lock your doors at night, don't you?"

I plaster a perpetual smile on my face in response to all of their comments and suggestions and questions.

I'm already sick of them. Is that wrong?

It's moments like this when I miss Amanda so bad the pain throbs like a fresh cut, still scarring over. Being an only child is too much pressure. My parents turn all of their attention and concern and energy onto my life and I feel responsible for filling something that's missing. To be two people. Sometimes it makes me feel small, as if Amanda and I were one person, and now I'm only half here. Amanda helped me to breathe and think and laugh and love. All these things that should come easily, that should be effortless, since her death, are some of my daily challenges. And even though I love my parents, it's always hard to be together because it's a reminder of what we lack. Now we're an odd number. And I know, deep down, that emptiness will always there, like a chasm between us.

While my parents drive to their hotel to check in, I panic. I run down to the Brew House and ask Lenny if she has seen Dylan.

"Not today," she tells me. I leave and jog down to Sage Street and knock on Dylan's door, but no one answers. I meet Cat just as she's closing the front door of the main house.

"Hey, is Dylan around?" I ask as she walks down the steps. She grins and points down the street and there's Dylan, halfway down the block, in corduroy shorts and a tank top, mowing somebody's lawn. I run down the sidewalk and when I meet her I see her shoulders are glistening with sweat and her face is flushed. My mind instinctively wants to get her in the shower, but now is not the time. She turns off the mower and smiles at me.

"It's a great day for a lemonade stand," she points out. "Want to try it? I bet we could make at least $2.50."

I shake my head and look down at the green lawn mower. I ask her if she's doing her good deed for the day but she informs me she's getting paid.

"We have a barter system. I get to take whatever I want from their vegetable garden," she says. She leans over the mower and whispers like she has a secret. "Hey, did you know vegetable gardens are proof that unicorns exist?"

I tell her I don't have time to hear this right now. She searches my eyes, which probably look desperate.

"What's wrong?" she asks. I drum my hands against my sides. I know this is a gamble. I know my mom will fall in love with her. I know Dylan will remind her of Amanda, in all the best ways. But, in my gut, I feel like she needs it. We all need it.

"I have a huge favor to ask," I say.

***

At my game, I see my parents sitting behind first base with a cluster of other parents and I notice Dylan has wriggled her way between them. My parents are wearing matching UNM T-shirts with my last name and number on the backs. Dylan's wearing her stone-washed jean jacket. For the first time, I'm relieved to see her in it. This is the Dylan I love, the girl that's so far off the normal spectrum that psychology needs a new term to define her.

I glance over my shoulder throughout the game and see my mom laughing. It's such an unusual expression for her to wear: happiness. It makes me smile and I know this was the right decision. I can't keep Dylan all to myself. You need to share your greatest gifts so other people can appreciate them, too.

Dylan

I spend the first few innings observing Gray's parents with fascination. I want to give them a trophy for conceiving Gray because he's perfect, but I think they're a little conservative for that kind of acknowledgement. I notice he inherited the best features of his parents; he has his mom's eyes—large and clear blue with long, dark lashes. He also has her wide mouth and smile. He has his dad's dark hair, athletic build and laugh and my favorite part of all, his sarcastic sense of humor. His mom is quiet, more observant and relaxed while his dad is outspoken and opinionated. His dad critiques and judges every play of the game and his mom is more patient and lighthearted. I think Gray is a blend of all these things, but in the best ways.

I turn to Clair and decide to get right to point. We've known each other almost an hour. It's time to open up about my future plans with her son.

"Clair, there's something you should know." She turns to me and raises her eyebrows. "I'm going to marry your son someday," I tell her. She stares back at me and she doesn't look surprised. More amused. She looks out on the pitcher's mound, where Gray's checking a first base player over his shoulder before he winds up for a throw.

"Have you discussed this plan with Gray?" she asks. I shake my head and tell her the timing isn't right.

"I just want you to know my intentions," I say.

We're quiet for a few seconds and I try to guess her thoughts: *Why do you want to marry my son? Do you want a big wedding? Who are you, exactly?* I notice her staring at my jean jacket with concern.

"Well, if you're going to be my daughter-in-law, maybe you and I should go shopping tomorrow."

I take a bite of my hotdog and the ketchup spills over the bun. "Shopping?" I ask, like we're not speaking the same language.

She nods. "Do you know how to get to the mall?"

"Oh, is there a mall here?" I ask with my mouth half-full.

She laughs. "You don't know?" she asks with unbelieving surprise.

We both turn to cheer when Gray strikes out two batters in a row to close out the sixth inning. I decide watching Gray play baseball is becoming my favorite pastime. Life doesn't get much better than hotdogs and sunshine and gazing out at a green field full of tan, athletic guys in tight pants.

"So, what do you think?" she asks.

I cough because, really, I'm thinking about her son's ass.

"About what?" I ask.

"Tomorrow?" she says. "Shopping."

I look in her eyes and they're hopeful and beaming and they're eyes that I love more than the world. I tell her I'll compromise and go shopping but only if we can stick to local spots, no malls. I explain to Clair that I try to be open-minded in life, but I have an aversion to the mall. She asks why and I explain that maybe in a past life, I was robbed or kidnapped in one because they freak me out.

"The people inside all look pale and unhealthy and shuffle around like zombies," I tell her. "They stare straight ahead, unblinking, like they're waiting for the world to end." I start to ramble because she's smiling and just like Gray's smile, it fires me up.

"The kiosk workers are terrifying," I say. "They stand in front of their booths like Nazis and insist your life won't be complete unless you own nail buffers, cuticle cutters, peppermint foot cream, clip-on hairpieces, or those neck rests filled with rice. Although I have to admit," I say, "I do enjoy the glazed nuts that come in those cone-shaped cups. That booth isn't so bad."

Clair shakes her head. "Amanda would have loved you," she tells me.

***

The next morning, Clair picks me up and takes me to an outdoor shopping area in Uptown. While we drive, she informs me that the boys are golfing. She says today is all about me. I wait for the words.

"I'm going to give you a makeover," she says with a wide smile. I manage a weak grin in return. My greatest fear for the day is confirmed. She's on a mission to turn me into her fashion project, a goal many people have made and failed miserably. I'm about to refuse, but her perfect smile, Gray's smile, makes me change my mind. I realize that this day really isn't about me. It's about her.

She pulls me into the first clothing store we pass and practically forces me into a yellow sundress. Clair insists if she had my body when she was my age, she would flaunt it, not hide it.

"But I'm not trying to hide it," I explain outside the dressing room. "I just want to be comfortable."

Clair ushers me inside the dressing room and I throw the sundress over my head. I walk out with a half-cocked grin on my face because I'm too tall to wear a sundress. I look like a dandelion.

"I don't think so," I say.

Clair adjusts the straps and tells me to relax my shoulders because I'm standing stiff and rigid and it doesn't do much for the look. The retail worker, who is about Clair's age, swears the dress is made for me. I raise my eyebrows.

"No dress was made for me," I assure them as I check out my reflection in three full length mirrors. Dresses are made for women with curves.

Clair tells me it's perfect. "Dylan, for such a gorgeous girl you need to show off your figure. Believe me, Gray will love it."

I perk up at this. These are the words that win me over. *Gray will love it.*

Clair insists on buying the yellow sundress for me and I feel guilty that she's paying $50 for something that feels like I'm wearing a drafty bed sheet. She tells me she'll only buy it if I promise to wear it the rest of the day. I agree on buying a pair of heeled sandals to go with it.

I am such a girl.

Now that I've broken the gift-giving seal, it can't be stopped. The next thing I know, I'm pulled into a makeup boutique and Clair and a makeup artist attack my face with sharp tweezers and pointy lip pencils and other scary instruments. I squeeze my hands around the seat of my chair until my knuckles are white and pray they won't poke an eye out. Gray owes me, big time.

I relent and for the next hour, I get my first makeover. My mom tried to do this with me dozens of times, but gave up, resigned to the fact she had a mutant daughter that wasn't into makeup and clothes shopping. Instead she settled on splurging with my little sister, who happily made up for both of us.

When they finish, they rotate my chair around until I'm facing a large mirror. I blink back at my reflection. My skin is all one even tone and it actually shimmers. My cheekbones look higher and have defined angles. My eyes look twice as big, my lashes twice as long and thick. I reach my hand up and brush my fingertip against my long lashes as if they aren't mine. I don't look like Dylan right now. I look like a Christie or a Connie. Maybe a Candy.

Clair claps her hands like this moment has made her entire year worthwhile. Then she glances at my hair.

"When's the last time you got a haircut?" she asks. I pick up a chunk of my hair and remember my sister trimmed it before I left for Europe, because she claimed it looked like a rat's nest.

"Maybe a year ago," I say.

Both of the women wince and I know what stop is next on the agenda.

What begins as a cut ends up being four inches hacked off with all these choppy layers around my face that the hairdresser promises will "frame" my bone structure, whatever that means. She insists my dark hair washes out my complexion, so she dyes it a caramel brown and adds blond highlights. She pulls on my hair for twenty minutes and tells me she's ironing it which scares me and I wonder why it isn't melting. I stare at myself in the mirror. My face is painted with color, I'm wearing a yellow sundress and now I have blond highlights to match it. My hair's brushed smooth and straight. No frizzies. No snarls.

"I look like—"

"A woman," Clair says. "I can't wait to see what Gray thinks."

"He won't recognize me," I say. I don't even recognize myself. Even though I appreciate all Clair's done, it's a little scary. As if I just transformed.

Gray

I see my parents at the game, but no Dylan. Maybe she and my mom didn't hit it off. I'm a little surprised, but it might be for the best. My mom gets attached too easily and Dylan's too temporary.

After the game my parents walk down to the field to meet some of my teammates, and I stop to sign autographs for a pack of kids swarming around the dugout. I head back to the field where a bunch of the players and family members are congregating. A few reporters are taking interviews. Coach Clark comes over to shake hands with my parents. He and my dad start discussing the game and my mom grabs my arm.

"Gray, aren't you even going to acknowledge Dylan?" she asks.

"What?" I ask. I look around for Dylan's jean jacket or her messy hair pulled back in a ponytail. Then, someone standing right next to me lightly hits me on the side of the head. I stare at this tall, gorgeous woman and finally recognize her. But it isn't Dylan. It's like her supermodel twin sister. I do remember seeing her now, in the stands during the game, but I figured she was somebody's girlfriend. Turns out, she's my girlfriend.

"Holy shit," I yell. My dad and Coach Clark both stop talking and regard me carefully. Then, they regard Dylan. A few other people turn to stare. I notice Travis gawking at her, clearly as surprised as I am.

"Gray, watch your mouth," my mom scolds me.

I just stare at her. My Dylan. She's wearing a…and her hair's even…what the?

"What happened to you?" I ask.

Dylan frowns. It's the most gorgeous frown I've ever seen in my life. She looks down at the ground, through eye lashes I never knew were so long.

"I know," she says and blushes, and I'm amazed she's the only girl who gets embarrassed when she looks beautiful. "It's lame."

"I gave Dylan a makeover," my mom says with a proud grin.

I don't believe it. "Did you have to drug her first?"

"I was kidnapped and forced to spend a day on Planet Girl," Dylan says.

She wraps her arms around her chest like she's trying to cover herself up. My mom squeezes her shoulders. "Doesn't she look beautiful?"

Dylan shakes her head. She meets my eyes and hers are magnified and sexy and it ties my stomach in a knot. "They curled my eye lashes with this scary torturing device—"

"We got lunch afterwards," my mom interrupts.

"They spent forty-five minutes ladling my hair—"

"Layering Dylan, it's called layering," my mom says.

I grin and I can't take my eyes off of her. I do the only thing I can, the only response that feels natural, even with my parents and Coach Clark and half my teammates standing right there. How often does your wildest fantasy come true?

"Amazing," I say and lean in and kiss Dylan full on the lips.

Gray

She's changing too fast and it's starting to worry me. She's always been a prism to me. She's meant to break light apart so you can see all the colors it's composed of. Now she's starting to cloud up. Blur.

The most recent shock is that she bought a cell phone. The gallery owners insisted she get one, so she can stay in touch with clients. Then, Liz gave her a purse to keep her cell phone in. She named her cell phone Frank. She named her automated voicemail service Jackie. Frank and Jackie, she claims, are her business partners. She also tells me that Frank and Jackie are married and live in Australia on an emu farm. It's twisted.

The phone scares her when it rings. She explains she hates any electrical device that beeps unexpectedly. I had to teach her how to answer it. She's yet to actually call anyone on it. Too many buttons to press, she says. I'm realizing she's pretty anti-technology. She won't even update her ancient camera.

She meets me Monday afternoon after class. I'm walking with Todd and Liz and I see her down the sidewalk. It's easy to recognize Dylan in the crowd because she's a head taller than most of the girls and the streaks of blond in her hair have a fiery, golden sheen in the sun. Dylan styles her hair now. It's never messy or tousled or pulled back in a ponytail. It's always parted on the side and usually tucked behind one ear.

She half runs, half skips when she sees us. She trips on her last jump and stumbles into my arms.

"Graceful," I say between laughs.

"Can you play?" she asks me.

I nod and tell her we don't have practice tonight. We had meetings and an early practice this morning. Dylan's mouth drops open.

"You have all day off?"

"Technically."

We stop at the sidewalk while a cargo train slowly passes, blocking our way across the street.

"I can barely wrap my mind around this. I have all day with you. We need to celebrate. We need to do something monumental."

"Calm down, Dylan," Liz says. "You're way too easily excited." I narrow my eyes at Liz for saying this.

"I'll do whatever you want," I tell Dylan, because her face is the brightest I've seen it in weeks.

"It has to be something we've never done before. Something that we'll remember forever." She looks around at us for inspiration.

Liz thinks about this. "Todd and I are registering for wedding gifts today," she offers. I look at Todd and he plasters a smile on his face like he shares her enthusiasm. I offer him a grin that's more out of sympathy.

Dylan turns to me for a better idea and I point to the train that's passing.

"I dare you to jump into one of those empty train cars."

Her eyes widen at the dare and she looks over at the tracks. "Really?"

"Sure," I say. "Ride it for the day and tell me all about it when you get back."

Dylan takes a flying leap off of the sidewalk and before I blink, her butt's in the air and she's pulling her legs up into the open door of an empty car. Todd, Liz and I stare at her as the train slowly inches away.

"Dylan, what are you doing?" Liz yells. "That's insane."

"Come on." Dylan ushers us forward with her hands. I walk along the train to keep up with her.

I spread my arms out in defeat. "Dylan, I was joking," I say.

She sits stubbornly in the open door and lifts her chin. The train whistles loudly and I keep up pace with Dylan's compartment. She swings her feet back and forth like a little kid on a carnival ride. I make a mental note to never dare this girl to do anything again. It all backfires.

I pass people on the sidewalk and see a few people from class I recognize. I wince as I notice Amber McCafrey with her sidekick Mel, standing near the curb, watching me.

"Oh, I get it," Dylan yells. "You're scared." I refuse to take the bait she's throwing out.

"That's right. Now get down from there."

"No."

"Dylan!"

She lies down on her side and tosses her hair back over her shoulder. "I wonder what it'd be like to have sex in one of these," she says, lowering her voice.

That's all the motivation I need. Before I can think another rational thought, I throw my backpack in the open door and heave myself up on the train, just as it picks up speed.

"You're nuts," I hear Todd yell in the distance and I lean down to wave at him and see Liz shaking her head with disapproval. A crowd of students have gathered along the sidewalk and a few people applaud. Dylan waves like she's a beauty pageant winner sitting on a parade float.

I turn and examine our traveling accommodations. There's a layer of straw on the floor. The walls are made up of flat, wood beams coarsely nailed together and painted a brownish-red. The train car is abandoned, except for a few stacks of hay in a shaded back corner. It smells like wood and dirt and the car shakes and squeaks over the tracks as we head away from campus. We watch the trail of people grow tinier in the distance.

"What do we do now?" I ask Dylan. She leans against one side of the open car door and I lean against the other.

"The sex thing was a joke," she says. "I don't have condoms."

The train's rumbling and shaking and vibrating and it's definitely turning me on. My eyes trail down her body. I meet her gaze under the rim of my baseball cap and smile.

"There are other ways to have sex, you know," I point out.

Dylan smirks and takes a gulp from her water bottle.

"Can I go down on you?" I ask.

She chokes on the water and it drips down her chin. She wipes it up with her hand and stares at me to see if I'm joking.

"Right now?" she asks. "You're a freak."

I nod at the compliment, turn my baseball cap backwards and pull Dylan into the back of the car without any more persuasion.

Dylan

I throw my leg lazily over the edge of the train car and lean against the side of the door. A long, contented sigh escapes from my chest. I'm so relaxed I could slide right off the train and melt all over the ground. The moving air awakens all my senses and the only sound I can hear is the grinding metal wheels of the train meeting the iron tracks. In the back of the car, Gray is still picking straw off his clothes.

"You're missing the scenery," I say as Gray scoots next to me.

"No I'm not," he says and kisses my neck, sliding his arms around my waist. He dangles his legs next to mine and we both look out to investigate our new surroundings. Far outside of Albuquerque, we have a view of a wide desert, the ground muted in dull tans and browns. Cliffs rise in the distance, their deep crevices shaded from the sun and making them look rippled. We pass desolate farmyards and a herd of cattle grazing close to the tracks. Small trickles of flowers and plants dot the landscape. I ask Gray what they are and he points out the green sagebrush and the creosote bushes. He tells me the plants with long, scrawny stalks and spiny leaves are agaves. He points out another plant, called a yucca, that looks like a miniature palm tree.

We share a picnic of fruit punch, crackers, nectarines and trail mix. We lay our small lunch out and slowly savor

the food and the sun and the rickety motion of the train
while a sleepy horizon passes by. I have everything I need
right here, in this moment.

I set the food aside and rest my head on Gray's lap.
He's sitting against the side of the door, eating a nectarine.
I wipe some juice off his chin with my finger before it
drips and he catches my hand in his and licks the juice off
my finger. He runs his warm hand over my forehead and
through my hair. His touch makes it hard to keep my legs
still. He brushes hair out of my eyes as the wind picks it up
around me.

"This was a good idea," he says.

He hands me the nectarine. I take the last couple bites
and nod.

"I'm glad we both appreciate white trash dates," I say.

Gray laughs and grabs the red pit out my hand and
throws it out on the desert ground. I sit up and lean my
head against his shoulder.

"I love you," I say.

"Why is that, exactly?" he asks. He gives me this
patient look, as if I'll need time to answer this. But I
automatically know.

"There are three things I look for in a person. And
you're the only person I've met in the world that has all of
them."

Gray waits for me to continue.

"First, you're always in the moment. You're not trying
to be ten places at once. You don't have to be glued to
your cell phone and texting your friends every two
seconds. It seems like people only feel important when
every second of their life is packed. They're always trying
to plan for tomorrow and they miss out on things
happening in front of them."

"That's a good one," he says.

"Second, you're real. You don't try to candy-coat life. You don't try and fix everything. You don't try to pretend life's perfect. Even if it means letting yourself be miserable or angry or upset. That's so stressful to me, to try and act my way through life instead of just relaxing and being myself."

He nods. I look out at a row of scrubby bushes with pink flowers blooming in the sun.

"Third, you let me stop and take pictures."

Gray creases his eyebrows together. "That's your third thing?"

"And most important." I say. "You let me be who I am. So many people ask me why I need to take pictures all the time. Why I'm staring at something they can't see. It's like I have to apologize for having eyes. But you've never rushed me. I'm at my best around you. You're my nova. You light me up."

Gray

The train slows down as it passes a railroad crossing, almost four hours later, and we take our exit opportunity. We jump down to the dusty ground and watch our red, wobbly car disappear down the track. The air is so still around us it feels like the earth has stopped moving.

I take out my phone, which I realize is dead and of course Dylan's doesn't have Internet. I use it to dial Lenny's number. When she answers, I tell her I'm stranded.

"You're stranded?" she asks. "What happened? Did your car break down?"

I stare at the train still visible in the distance. "Um, not exactly," I say.

"Where are you?"

"I'm not sure," I say. I look around at what appears to be a ghost town. There's an RV park down the road, with two ramshackle trailers parked in a field overgrown with weeds and scraggly shrubs. Everything looks deserted. Dylan's off taking pictures of a dilapidated shed—she's no help at all.

"I need a bit more detail than that, Gray," she says. "Is there a street sign or something?" I walk down the road and look for anything, even a landmark that could pinpoint our location. There's an old, brick church with the doors and windows all boarded up. I tell her to get online and look up St. Mary's Church.

Dylan wanders back over to my side. "We passed a town called Magdalena a while back," she offers. I tell this to Lenny.

"Where the hell is that?" she asks.

"Southern-ish?" I guess.

Lenny's typing on her computer. "How did you end up there?" she asks. I explain Dylan kidnapped me and forced me to ride on a cargo train with her for a few hours.

"He dared *me*," Dylan yells into the phone.

"I'm not seeing any church listing, Gray," Lenny says.

Dylan tugs on my fingers. "Tell her to look up Bill's General Store, it's right down the street."

Lenny looks it up and I hear an annoyed groan. "You're over two hours away!"

I laugh at this. "Please, Lenny? We're stranded."

"Serves you right."

"I'll give you gas money."

"Damn right. And your *Spinal Tap* shirt."

My jaw drops open at this outlandish demand. "I can't believe you're taking advantage of me right now."

She isn't apologetic. "What'll it be?"

"No way, not the shirt. I'll buy you beer for a month."

"You're not even twenty-one you idiot, and you have a crappy fake. How are you going to buy me beer? *Spinal Tap* or no ride."

I tighten my lips together. "You can *borrow* it until I buy you your own shirt."

"Deal. Try not to get kidnapped out there."

She hangs up and I give the phone back to Dylan.

"We have some time to poke around downtown," I say like we're in a tourist hub surrounded by souvenir shops. Dylan and I examine the road in each direction. We appear to be on a main street of sorts. There's a broken-down mill, half caved in. I tell Dylan it must have been a mining town. Probably zinc or iron. We walk down the street until we come to the last building in sight, a brick warehouse with a crumbling roof and boarded up windows.

"Not a strong local economy," I observe. Dylan's busy taking pictures of old, faded signs and cracks and weeds growing up through holes in the brick wall of the abandoned warehouse. She asks me to pose in a few of her shots. I frown in front of the barricaded church and look disappointed next to the closed general store. I take a few pictures of Dylan. She holds her face in her hands as she sits in front of the boarded-up warehouse door, like she's modeling for high school portraits. She lies seductively on her side in front of a stack of car tires. She twists a few weeds into her hair and holds a bouquet of tumbleweed. I get a close-up. It's priceless.

We walk back towards the church and I sit in the middle of the road and stare up at it. Dylan sits next to me and takes out a bag of crackers.

"I don't think I've ever seen a church closed down," I say.

Dylan nods. "It's not a good sign when God goes out of business." She nibbles on a few crackers and stretches her legs out. "How long would you say we have to wait?" she asks.

"About an hour," I say and pop a cracker in my mouth.

"That's a perfect amount of time to write the history of this church," she says.

I look at her and raise an eyebrow. "The history of this place?" I ask.

She nods and flashes me a smile. It makes my heart jump. "I'll start," she offers. "The church was built in the year 250 B.C., when King Archibald the 11th ruled the land."

I study the old church. "The king had only one son," I add, "who was born with leprosy." Dylan smiles and grabs a handful of crackers. "But back then, they didn't know what leprosy was, so the King thought his son was possessed by demons and banished him from the castle to live in this church."

"Where he was locked up in the basement until he healed. He was never allowed to have visitors," Dylan says.

A neon orange sun sets behind the old ghost town. Dylan still has weeds tied in her hair and dust all over her clothes. I smile and tell her she's more herself today.

She leans back on her hands. "It's weird, but I feel the most at home when I'm roaming." I nod because the more time I get to spend with her, the more I witness how this is true.

Suddenly, Dylan's phone rings and it makes her scream with surprise. I almost jump off the ground.

"You really need to stop doing that," I say.

"Sorry," she says, and picks up her phone. "It's the gallery." She answers it and while she listens her eyes light up.

"What?" she asks. "He's interested in hiring *me*?" She laughs and listens for another minute and something in her face changes. Her smile turns to disappointment.

"Oh," she says, the excitement slipping out of her voice. "I don't know if I can commit to that. Yeah, if I'm interested I'll call him. Thanks so much for the reference, Mary." She hangs up and looks out at the street.

"What happened?" I ask.

"A travel photographer came into the gallery today," she says. "He's looking for an assistant and he liked my work, so Mary recommended me. He's interested in hiring me."

"Are you serious?" I ask. "That's great."

"The shoot's in Australia," she says.

"Isn't that on your wish list?" I ask.

She nods. "It's number one on my wish list."

"Then call him, what are you waiting for?" She looks at me as if I'm forgetting something. I start to register what's wrong.

"How long is the job for?" I ask her.

"He has a three month shoot scheduled, starting next month, but he wants to stay for a year if he can get enough work."

I nod at this news and my own excitement for her deflates. One year?

"I'm not going to call him," she decides and shakes her head quickly.

"Dylan—"

"It isn't meant to be," she says. She looks back at the church and continues with our story and I watch her closely while she talks. I feel a pang of guilt in my chest. We're going to destroy her if we keep her here. It's like holding someone hostage.

So why am I allowing her to stay?

We don't get halfway through the story before we hear a car coming towards us, Nine Inch Nails blaring out the open windows. We watch Lenny's blue Toyota speed up to us and take our time to finish off the last of our crackers. I brush a few crumbs off my shirt.

Lenny rolls to a stop and pokes her head out to glare at us.

"Did you find it okay?" I ask. She narrows her eyes at me, clearly annoyed.

"I just have one question," she says.

Dylan and I look at each other and then back at Lenny.

"Are you two planning on getting married someday?" she asks.

My face heats up. "Why?" I ask.

"Because I'm officially worried for your children," she says.

Gray

A week later, Todd becomes my first friend to officially hit marriage status. Scary. Getting married is probably the lamest thing you can do in college. College marks your pre-adulthood years, where you're meant to screw up on a daily basis. This includes embracing your curfew-free schedule, studying only when you experience a lag in social engagements, and enjoying drunken debauchery with your fellow peers. Not discussing matrimony dates and picking out dishware and sheet sets.

Bubba and I hide out on the front porch to escape the overbearing estrogen levels concentrated in our living room. The Liz Wedding Party is currently spread out watching the DVD of their ceremony. I've already seen it. Twice. Bubba's chewing and he hocks a thick wad of brown spit off our front porch into the grass. The stream barely misses my shoulder.

"Dude, that's sick," I say.

Bubba shakes his head. "Not as sick as the freak show happening in my living room right now. Since when did our house become the headquarters of Future Housewives of America?"

Just as he says this there's a chorus of laughter inside, all high pitched squeals. Bubba shudders.

"If I ever, even consider getting married, will you do me a favor?" he asks. He looks at me with serious eyes and I nod. "Shoot me in the head?" he asks. "Poison me, knock me unconscious, anything. Just talk me out of it."

I chuckle at this and finger-pick a few strings on my guitar. "It couldn't be that bad," I say. "I hear it's a pretty common relationship move." A long stream of sighs escapes from all the girls inside.

"And half of those moves end in divorce," Bubba points out. He glances in the window. "I just can't believe Todd got married in the middle of the season. They're not even living together until the fall. What's the point of getting married if you can't at least bang each other on a daily basis?"

"Love makes you do crazy things," I say.

"Tell me about it. Look at Miles. Pretending to like mediocre chick bands that play covers of other mediocre chick band's music." He shakes his head with disappointment.

"Cat's good, you have to admit," I say. I decide to call him on his own behavior.
"What about you?" I ask.

"What about me?"

"I know you've been helping out at Lenny's place. She told me you built a fence in their backyard and fixed their kitchen sink. Since when are you a repair man?"

"It's just her and her mom right now," Bubba says. "They need a hand."

"See, even you have a sensitive side."

He eyes Dylan inside, sitting with a couple of Liz's friends. They're putting finishing touches on the gifts for the dinner party this weekend. They're stuffing white, sparkly bags with music mixes and chocolates and tying white bows on the top.

"Dylan has surprised me more than anyone," he says.

I stare at him and ask him what he means.

"She turned herself upside down, flipped herself inside out. I don't even recognize her anymore. She's like this whole different person than she was a few months ago."

I follow his gaze to Dylan. She's sitting on the rug with the other girls and she fits in. She dresses like them. She's neat and groomed and accepted—and almost indistinguishable.

Bubba stands up and stretches.

"Don't get me wrong, she looks good," he says. He slaps his hand against my shoulder and grins. "It's just nice to know we're all idiots when it comes to love," he says, and disappears inside the house.

I sit on the chair outside and I watch Dylan. Even though her hair is styled and her outfit is brighter and her lips sparkle, something about her has dimmed.

Bubba's right. She transformed. All for me.

I watch her laugh when the other girls laugh. She swoons at all the right times like she's following along with a script someone passed out. It's too programmed. Too normal. She never wanted to be normal. She called it stifling, and I fell in love with her for being so extreme.

I stand up and walk down the street and try to clear my head. I think about Amanda and wonder what I would do if someone tried to narrow her horizons, if someone cut her dreams short or controlled her. I would have stepped in and forced sense into her, even if it made her mad, even if she hated me for it. Because I loved her too much to let her settle. The people that love you have the responsibility to look out for you, to see your potential. I knew the difference Amanda would have made in the world. I saw the glow of optimism she showered around her that needed to be spread out. Dylan's like that. So, how can I let this happen?

A few raindrops start to fall and they're cold against my skin. It gives me the chills. I stand in the street and look up at a black sky. There's only one thing left to do.

Dylan

I observe Gray across the room. Even though I broke down his walls, a few beams and studs are still standing. There are nails sticking out of them and I snag myself on them once in a while. I trip over some of the fallen beams that lay scattered on the floor.

I still can't figure him out sometimes. Maybe that's why I'm so fascinated by him. I never know what to expect.

I watch the wedding party unfolding around me, but I feel like a wallflower, like I'm inside a movie set and this is all a dress rehearsal. This can't be real. Have I really hit the marriage zone? How can people get married when they're twenty? And if this is such a joyous occasion, why do I feel sorry for them?

It's strange to think that I'm coming back to this place. These friends will all be waiting for me. I've never returned to a place I've lived before. Why go back to something known, when there's so much waiting to be discovered? But all I have to do is look at Gray to be reassured why I'm doing this.

I try to be happy about this decision, but there's something in my gut that tightens. A little voice is questioning me because I never thought I'd put my dreams on hold. For anybody. I never thought I would change myself for another person.

I watch guys who are used to living in grass stains and dirty clothes all standing awkwardly in dress slacks and button up shirts. I grin at Miles, who succeeded in burning the collar of one of his dress shirts and melting two buttons off of another. I came to his rescue before he scorched shirt number three. I watch him stand next to Cat. They look mismatched standing next to each other. Miles is so clean cut and all-American, while Cat's in a flowing, long blue cotton dress that looks hand-made, a scarf tied around her hair. But their differences complement each other. You can never guess who people are going to fall for. Love is more like an accident than a plan. It's more of a question than an answer.

I turn and see Lenny standing with a frown on her face. She's wearing a black dress that she keeps pulling and yanking down. She stands awkwardly in her black heels, like she's wishing they were boots. The only time her face relaxes into a smile is when Bubba's at her side, which is most of the time.

I sigh as I look around. Weddings are supposed to be happy so why do I feel like something tragic is in the air? Is it because Gray's been avoiding me tonight? We came to the party together, but other than our entrance, you wouldn't know we're together. He's always on the opposite side of the room. He wears a tight, forced smile instead of his usual lazy grin. It's part of his outfit—uncomfortable and constricting, like underneath he's unraveling. I want to ask him what's wrong, but I can't get him alone.

All around the room I'm reminded of love, so why do I feel like it's being yanked out from under my feet?

Gray

I've been avoiding Dylan. It's difficult to look at her. I watch Travis flirt with her like I'm not standing in the same room. At least he's smart enough to keep his hands off of her. I watch Coach Clark talk to her and I hear him laugh as she gestures wildly with her hands. She leaves a trail of smiles everywhere she goes. Guys give her second glances. Most of the girls stare with a jealous edge to their eyes. This is the most entertaining thing for me. If only they knew the real Dylan, the one that scampers around in holey socks and tattered clothes and gets more out of the dirt on the ground than the clothes in any store. But they don't see Dylan this way. Because this isn't her.

Suddenly she's next to me and I feel her soft hand crawl inside mine. I look down at her and she's studying me.

"I have a theory," she says.

"Does it have something to do with changing the legal marriage age to at least twenty-one?" I ask.

She shakes her head. "You've been hiding in the back corner all night. There could only be three possible reasons for this."

I straighten my back. "Which are?"

"That you're either avoiding me because I'm almost as tall as you in these shoes and it makes you feel emasculated."

"A woman can never be too tall," I inform her.

"Or you have IBI," she says.

"IBI?"

"Insane butt itch. It's okay. It happens to everybody. It's usually because you don't wipe thoroughly after you go to the bathroom."

I roll my eyes.

"Don't be embarrassed," she says. "It always happens at the worst possible moments. You just need to find a corner where you can scratch without being too obvious."

"Have I ever told you how classy you are?"

"Third," she pauses and leans in close to me. "There's something on your mind."

I look in her eyes and swallow. The party is dwindling down now, and I feel suffocated in all this packaged happiness. I ask her if she wants to go for a walk. She nods and while she changes out of her heels into a pair of sandals, I give Miles my car keys and tell him we're walking home. He regards me for a moment because he sees the stress in my eyes but I turn away before he gets a chance to ask. I follow Dylan out of the party and I have to focus on breathing because it's the only thing that's making my legs work.

***

We walk down the street and we're both quiet. There's no way to transition. There's no easy way to say it. So I get straight to the point. Make it fast. It will be easier this way.

"Dylan, I want to say goodbye to you tonight."

I feel her watching me and I know she's registering something, but she tests me. "You mean you don't want to sleep over?"

I take a deep breath. "I mean, I think you should leave Albuquerque."

She stops walking and faces me. "I haven't bought a plane ticket yet," she says. "Besides, why does it matter when I leave? I'm coming back—"

She cuts herself off. I stare at her and she reads my eyes.

"Oh, my gosh. You don't want me to come back, do you? That's what you're trying to tell me."

I nod. She stares at me and the silence of the night presses against us. A car drives up the road, so we move onto the sidewalk. Dylan's still absorbing my words.

"How long have you felt like this?" she asks.

"Since you announced your crazy plan to live here," I say.

She chooses her words slowly. "Why do you want me to leave?" she asks.

"I barely recognize you anymore. Everyone thinks you look great and your life couldn't be better, but I've never seen you more unhappy. The only time you've been yourself in the last month is when we were riding on the train. *Getting out of town.*"

She looks down at the ground. "Why don't you want me to come back next fall?"

"Because you're only doing it for me," I say. I turn and face her and I pray she'll understand. "I love you more than any of these people, but I don't want you to come back here."

"I am really confused right now," she says.

"You only think with your heart, Dylan," I tell her. "So I'm going to be your brain. Because you're about to make a huge mistake." I pause for a second before I try and explain this. "Don't you remember anything you said last summer? You told me you didn't want to live *my* life. You told me you'd have to pass up all your dreams and you'd resent me. Well, you're right. And if I let you stay now, *I'll* resent me."

I watch her face change. I know she agrees, but she's fighting it. "People say I'm selfish for always wanting to leave," she says.

"Selfish? Dylan, look at all the people you've changed in the last few months. Miles and Cat wouldn't be so happy. Lenny wouldn't have a new best friend and be starting nursing school this summer. You even brought down Toolshed's ego. Liz follows you around like a puppy. You made my mom smile more than I thought she was capable of. Look at all the people you've had an impact on and ask me again if you're selfish."

I see something like relief pass over her eyes. There's a small grin on her face. Just like that, I pumped life back into her. She really was fading.

"You need to call that photographer," I tell her. "You have to go Australia—you don't give up an opportunity like that."

Her smile grows. "You could always come with me," she says. "Or meet up with me when you have time off."

I shake my head. "We have completely different dreams. I don't have a mission to see the world. That's not my calling. I just try to make it one day at a time. But I'm not going to be the one who holds you back."

"You really mean it?"

I nod again. "Dylan, you're one of those rare people that has an endless supply of love. Don't use it all on me. It's like you said, it's your mission to spread yourself out. I can't keep you all to myself. I can't waste you."

She smiles. There's already a bouncier step to her walk. We turn the corner onto Sage Street and she squeezes my hand in hers. It makes me want to cry.

"So, what happens next? Are you going to get mad if we go a few months without seeing each other again?"

I shake my head again and my throat tightens, but I have to hold myself together. Just get it out. "It's over," I hear myself say. "We're over."

Her hand slips out of mine like water dripping off of something melting.

"Wait. Did you just break up with me?"

The words make me wince. I stare in her eyes, shaded in the darkness. The color in her face drains out. Her skin is the palest I've ever seen.

"You're breaking up with me," she says, again. I hear her breathe.

I look away from her face. I can't look at something I've broken. "This isn't meant to be. You shouldn't have to change your life for another person. You, of anybody, should get that."

"But you don't even want to stay in touch?" she asks, her voice uneven.

I shake my head.

Her voice trembles. "Why can't we be friends?"

Friends? I glare at her. She knows better than to ask me this. "I can't just be your friend. We tried that, remember? And I don't want you in my life for short bursts of time. I told you when you showed up here, *I can't do that*." My voice rises reflexively because I'm barely holding on right now.

"So, let me get this straight. I'm the love of your life. I'm the best thing that has ever happened to you, and you're throwing it all away?"

"I'm doing this for *you*," I argue, my voice rising again. She surprises me and shoves me like she's trying to wake me up out of some kind of trance. Then she shoves me again and I back up a few steps. I look at her and I'm angry now because her eyes are blurring with tears and it's all my fault.

"Don't do it," she says. "I love you. I don't want to break up. Ever. We can make it work."

She starts to really cry now, so hard she's shaking and I rub my hands over my face. My own eyes start to burn. I want to fix her. I wish I had all the right words.

"Dylan, the best thing I ever did was walk past you a year ago in that courtyard in Phoenix. You changed my life. And I'll never regret letting you go. But you need to let me go, too."

She chokes out her words and hangs her head. "What if I never see you again?"

"You're the one that always said to leave this to fate." I cup her cheek against my palm and stare into her eyes, magnified behind a pool of tears. "Don't ever change for anyone. Promise me?"

Tears are dripping off her chin. She covers her hands over her face and cries into them. I watch this angel I broke. A silver light falls over her and makes her skin look like stone, but I turn to walk away. I hate that this is my last image of her. It's not what I wanted at all. And I don't shed a tear. My voice never quavers. It's like somebody pumped lead into my heart and steel into my brain. I walk away like a machine. I keep moving before my thoughts make me collapse.

I don't dare look over my shoulder. I hear whimpering behind me. I need to hold it together. The sky's falling in around me. Stars are burning souls. Melting planets. Flying comets spiraling towards a crash landing. Clouds are ghosts. The moon is a lonely, unblinking eye.

I swear at the ground. Life is never a perfect story book. It isn't happily ever after or one fine day or love everlasting. It's twisted and warped and it peels and tears and your heart just becomes this piece of shredded fabric sewn over with patches.

I can hear people pass me on the sidewalk, but I can't see them. They're floating shadows. I feel the tears start to stab my eyes.

Not yet, Gray. Deep breaths. Hold it together. Just a little longer.

I turn at the next block. A drooping streetlight sprinkles a golden hue down a lifeless street.

A few more seconds. Hold on.

I pick up the pace and make it into the empty alley that leads to my house.

Okay. Now. Cry your eyes out.

Dylan

I drag myself out of bed the next morning to face a future
I never planned. To face a moment I don't belong in. I feel
like a stranger in my own skin. I turn on the bathroom
light and a glum, puffy eyed girl stares back at me. I barely
recognize her. She looks like she could be related to me.
The same eyes, the same chin and nose. The same freckles
and skinny, long neck. But she slipped into an identity that
doesn't fit her, like a pair of shoes that are too tight and
limit your movements. It isn't complementing, it's
constricting. But sometimes it's hard to see until someone
points it out.

I stare down at the pajamas that Liz gave me, a
matching cotton T-shirt and draw string shorts that are
perfect and pretty and plain. What was I doing? I look like
all of you now.

I glare back at my appearance and tighten my lips. I
almost lost my identity. I blend in. Why was I trying to
become one of you?

Why do some people try to trap me? Don't they get
that it's in my anatomy to fly?

I look down at the basket of makeup on the counter. I
don't want to hide behind anything. I don't want to
disguise my imperfections just because people tell me
they're flaws. I think they're what make me unique. My
blotchy skin. My boring hair. Don't try to make me

beautiful. I already am. And I don't want to be idolized for something so temporary as outward beauty. It never lasts.

I stare at this girl who has been crumbling for the past month. Who almost lost herself. I straighten my shoulders.

The first thing I do is wash her face, where a smudge of black mascara colors dark rings under her eyes. The next thing I do is grab a pair of scissors from the drawer and go to work at her hair. It's thick and I have to cut small sections at a time, but I eventually make my way around her head, throwing handfuls of long hair into the garbage and cutting until the ends fall short, just below her ears. It's jagged and uneven and it suits her. I grab a baseball cap I inherited from Gray, a red cap with the Lobo mascot decorating the front. I pull it over her forehead and it's soft and worn in. It hides the bags under her eyes from staying up half the night crying. I start to recognize her again.

I touch the ends of my messy, uneven hair spilling out from under the cap.

It's me. I'm back. It's been a while.

I throw all the makeup in the garbage and snap off the bathroom light. I pack up the rest of my clothes, but realize, as I'm folding, I don't want any of them. I throw the coordinated outfits, the trendy tanks, the cropped jeans, and the high heeled shoes, on a heap on top of the bed. I figure Catherine can find something to do with them. I decide to keep the dress Clair bought me. I genuinely like it, and it will always remind me of a generous heart. I get dressed in an old, baggy pair of jeans with a recent rip in one knee. I pull a yellow tank top over my head. It's soft and faded and perfect.

I walk down the sidewalk, squinting against the bright glare of the late morning sun. I wish it was rainy and cold, something better suited to my mood. All the sunshine and beauty and the smell of freshly cut grass makes my head pound. No one has the right to be happy today. Gray broke up with me. The world should mourn my broken heart, not rejoice in sunny, June weather. I frown at a shirtless guy mowing his lawn and want to say, "Hey, how can you just go on with life like that? Don't you realize my world just fell apart? And you're worried about your *lawn*?"

I try to live life one day at a time. Don't focus too far into the future; don't hang too closely to the past. But how can I live day to day without him? I can barely go ten minutes without thinking about him. A day, one whole, entire day is impossible. So I'll go moment by moment. One second at a time. One breath. That's what I'll have to do. And maybe I'll be okay.

I learned something today. I learned that the heart, our most vital organ, turns out to be our weakest link. It's scary to think something so necessary to sustain us, protected in a cradle of ribs and flesh and muscles, is so fragile, so easily broken.

I swing the door open to the Brew House and I can tell by Lenny's sympathetic face that she's already talked to Gray. She force feeds me coffee and a muffin and tells me I look terrible. I appreciate her honesty.

"What happened to your hair?" she asks as she stands next to the table and studies me.

"I tend to take out my emotional stress on either my nails or my hair," I tell her.

"Actually," she says. "I kind of like it. It's more you." I swallow down the hot coffee and begin writing farewell letters. Cat's out of town to play a show so I can't say goodbye to her in person. Liz is working today and the last thing I want to do is walk into her boutique looking like this. I'll give her a panic attack. I consider writing letters to Gray's roommates, even Travis, but I know when Gray shut me out of his life, it included his friends. When I'm done, I stand up and walk over to the counter.

"What are you going to do?" Lenny asks.

"I booked the first flight I could get on," I say in a voice that's so monotone it doesn't sound like me. "I leave in a few hours."

Lenny's quiet and she doesn't try to sugar coat my thoughts. That's what I love about her. You can just *be* around her. You don't have to wear a fake smile or say everything's fine because she knows. She's like Gray, she can see through the artificial masks so many people dress up in. She keeps it real, and there's a comfort in this.

I hand Lenny a stack of letters and ask her to hand them out. I tell her to keep up with Sunday night dinners. It's a great tradition.

She fidgets with the string of her apron. "Yeah, but it won't be the same. You were the one that made it happen."

"Liz can take my place," I say. Lenny looks down at her feet and slowly nods.

"Well, I'd say keep in touch but," Lenny starts.

"Yeah," I agree. It's not going to happen. Lenny surprises me and grabs me in a tight hug. She smiles at me, a warm, genuine smile.

"Good luck, Dylan" she says. "I'm really glad I got to know you." I nod and walk away without turning back.

I head downtown, my conscious state wavering somewhere between reality and a dream. I have three hours to kill before I need to be at the airport to catch my flight. So I do the only thing that comes naturally. I lift my camera to my eye and let my mind escape.

When I look through the lens, I look outside myself. And that's when I really start to see.

I turn down a shaded sidewalk to Lily Park and find a cluster of people sitting outside, enjoying the sunny afternoon. I walk around the outskirts of the park, watching people. I pass an older man talking on his cell phone. He looks about sixty and he's smiling. I notice the gorgeous laughter wrinkles around his eyes. I crouch down and just as he leans back and laughs, the light hits his face and I take a picture of his profile. Every wrinkle on his face curls up in the sunlight, like a face full of a thousand smiles. It makes some of the dark spots in my chest lighten. I grin and keep walking.

I notice a girl stretching out on a quilted blanket in the sun. She's highlighting a textbook page. Next to her is an opened spiral notebook with coffee stains on the paper. I stroll by and, over her shoulder, take a picture of the coffee stained notebook.

Across the street from the park, I see an old, rickety blue house with a white front porch that holds a green, swinging bench. The white paint of the porch is crackled and peeling, but in a warm way. In a way that makes it look used, loved, lived in, and worn in with movement and feet and bodies. It looks like home, so I steal a permanent image.

I study a man eating a sack lunch by himself on the sidewalk, alongside a utility truck. He's wearing steel-toed tan boots, and a yellow hard hat lies next to him. His face is deeply tanned. I notice his jeans, faded and streaked with heavy dirt. When he looks away, I click a picture of his dirty jeans, his strong, muscular arms resting on his knees.

I watch two young girls swing on a swing set and when they hit the highest point, where it looks like they could fly off into the sky, I snap a picture.

I notice a young woman and her son in another corner of the park. She's picking some of the wild daises that grow in the grass. She carries a handful and wraps one in her hair. She wears a long peasant dress over baggy jeans and her hair is tied back in a loose braid. I take her picture. Her little boy is running through the tall grass in nothing but his diaper, which is sagging halfway down his butt. He laughs as the breeze tickles his skin. I smile and when he turns to run back to his mother. I catch his leaping prance on film.

As I circle the park, the last thing I notice is an empty wooden park bench. A colorful mural is painted over it, a sky with clouds and a meadow of flowers. There are words painted on the bench in black letters that say, "Reserved for Dreamers." I stare down at the words and take a picture.

I finish up my roll of black and white film at this perfect park, with the perfect name. In that short amount of time, something is liberated. Something shifts. I'm me again, reintroduced, seeing people, forgetting myself, loving the moment, and living the moment, carefree.

I walk to the Desert Gallery, but it's closed so I leave my letter in a plastic bag and hang the bag on the doorknob. I also leave the black and white roll of film I took today, scribbling a note telling them to do whatever they want with the pictures. I write the name of this particular collection: *At Our Best.*

I hail a cab, but before I get in, I take one last look at the gallery, where a few of my prints still hang in the window display. I think about the day Gray brought me here, helped to show me my potential. I think about our kiss. I look at my roll of film, hanging in the plastic bag. I almost let this city trap me. I was settling to feel safe, to avoid taking a risk. This is dangerous because fear stunts your soul. And I'd much rather grow.

While the taxi creeps away from Albuquerque, I pull out a piece of paper Mary gave me, with the travel photographer's number. I starting dialing the digits and with each number I press, I feel lighter. I feel excited again—thrilled to be moving.

Maybe, I think, just maybe this is me, at my best.

Maybe Gray did me the biggest favor of all.

Maybe it's not the doors that open in our lives, but the doors that close that define us. That guide us. Because they force us to move on. Instead of thinking about what we lose, look at what we can gain. I know Gray closed this door to force me to open up all the other ones inside of me. Outside of me. Around me. And now I'm stepping through.

Gray

I throw a black suitcase in my trunk and slam the door closed. Lenny's smoking on the porch steps, watching me. Miles, Bubba and Todd have already left town for summer league teams all over the country. I'm playing in Nebraska.

I'm looking forward to a change of scenery. To the hot summer nights. To a field where I can control my actions everyday, where I can mentally escape. And to days where all that's expected of me is sleeping in and lifting weights. I know some guys on the team—I played against them this year—and a few of us are renting a house for the summer, downtown, close to the University. I know there will be parties and late nights and girls and memories to make. But I don't care about all that. I'm just ready for a long distraction.

Lenny jumps down from the steps when she sees I'm ready to go. She's wearing my *Spinal Tap* shirt, just to annoy me.

"When do you start classes?" I ask her. Her face lightens up and she tells me one week. I tell her she's the only person I've ever met who's excited about summer school. She just found out she's a finalist for a full scholarship and as long as her references follow through, she's in.

"You'll be busy," I say. She nods and even though we're not sentimental, I scoop her up in my arms and give her a hug. I pick her up off the ground because she's a good foot shorter than me. When I set her down there's something serious in her eyes.

"Don't lecture me on staying clean this summer," I say. "What happens in Nebraska stays in Nebraska."

"I'm the last person to lecture you," she says. "Besides, I still argue smoking pot makes you live longer." She takes something out of her back pocket. At first I think she's actually giving me weed, but it's an envelope, folded in half. She opens it and I see my name spelled out in unmistakable handwriting. I wrinkle my forehead and Lenny extends it to me.

"I wasn't sure if you were ready, that's why I waited to give it to you."

I stare down at it, but I don't take it. Lenny and I haven't talked about Dylan since the day I told her we broke up.

"When did she give it to you?" I ask. Lenny tells me Dylan stopped in the day she left. She tells me she wrote a few letters and asked Lenny to hand them out to people, since she was leaving town too fast to say goodbye.

She holds the envelope between us and I feel like so much of my life is folded up inside that stupid piece of paper. She's holding a slice of my heart there, a secret, a story. The greatest story I've ever experienced. I don't want to read it. I want to burn it. But, I grab it out of her hand.

"Thanks," I say. Lenny watches me shove it in my back pocket.

"Aren't you going to read it?" she asks.

I shrug and open my car door.

"It might give you some closure," she says.

I smirk. Closure. That's probably the most unrealistic word in the English vocabulary. It's up there with heartbreak, pain, loss, and abandonment, all these things that you're supposed to get over and mend and heal but really, do you ever get over those moments?

Do you ever forget your first love? So much stems from there, and your life will always be connected back to that person. The faintest trail of memories will always be there, like a map scarred into your mind.

I tell Lenny goodbye, get into my car, and start the engine. I slide a mix I made for the drive into the stereo. As I merge on the freeway, the envelope feels like a rock in my back pocket, so I pull it out. I roll down my window and I'm about to fling it out, but I stop. I tear through the paper and open up the folded note. There are only a few sentences written in her sloppy writing that I swear looks tear-stained and it makes my heart pinch in my chest to see it. I glance down quickly and read the writing as fast as I can to get it over with.

Dear Gray,
I understand. You were right. I need to keep moving. Thank you for loving me enough to help me realize it. You'll always make me shine. I hope you find your constant sun.
Love always,
Dylan

I take a deep breath and hold the letter between my fingers. Dylan will always be this butterfly in my eyes. Something beautiful I held long enough to be spellbound with what exists in the world. But the problem with butterflies is they flutter off, and you spend the rest of your time running and jumping after them and making an idiot out of yourself trying to catch them, only to come up empty handed and looking like a fool in the process. The point of it all is, they aren't meant to be caught, and you would feel guilty trying to contain them. They'll wither in your hands and suddenly you realize they're beautiful because they're free. They're meant to be wild. Unattainable. Like they belong in a fairytale.

I stare out at the sunny horizon. And I'm surprised because I'm waiting for tears or pain in my chest but, instead, something heavy is lifting. It isn't quite closure, but Lenny was right, I do feel better. I'm relieved Dylan understood so quickly. That she forgives me. In a way, this sets me free. So I throw the white piece of paper out of my car window and it sails like a bird into the wind.

In the very back of my mind, there's a tiny sliver of hope. Maybe we'll meet again someday. Maybe Dylan's been right all along. We can't force it. We need to leave this one to fate.

I turn up my stereo to Bob Dylan singing, *Don't Think Twice*. The lyrics sum up my life. Like magic. The harmonica wails and I focus my eyes ahead and set my destination on the horizon, and, always, on the forever glowing desert sun.

Readers:

Do you want Gray and Dylan's story to continue? Well good news, there's more to come!

Be sure to read the first book in the series, *First Comes Love*, and keep your eye out for the third and final book in the Gray and Dylan saga, *Finally, Forever*.

For more information about Katie Kacvinsky and her books, check out her website:

www.katiekacvinskybooks.wordpress.com

Acknowledgements:

Thanks to my agent, Helen Breitwieser. You are my compass. Thanks for loving this book and helping to steer it into publication. Thanks to my amazing content editor (and sister), Sarah Moeser. I had a blast working with you on this manuscript. When we weren't exchanging movie and music recommendations (or obsessing over how much we both loved *Magic Mike*), we were talking about *Second Chance*. Thanks to Jennie Bartlemay for being a copy editing wizard (yes, she is seriously part wizard). I also need to thank Julia Richardson, my editor from Houghton Mifflin Harcourt. She read this manuscript and made some wonderful suggestions that helped shape the story. Thanks to Damaris Cardinali for basically being my publicist for this book. I heart you. Thanks to Graham for getting me outside every day, to Kaleb for reminding me what is most important, and to Adam, for making this all possible.